THE BAND ON THE PROM

First published in: 2015

ISBN: 978-1-84524-234-3

Cover design: Eleri Owen
Cover photograph by J. A. Jones

Published by Gwasg Carreg Gwalch,
12 Iard yr Orsaf, Llanrwst, Wales LL26 0EH
tel: 01492 642031
fax: 01492 641502
email: books@carreg-gwalch.com
website: www.carreg-gwalch.com

The Band on the Prom

The Story of the Llandudno Town Band from 1900

Susan M. Wolfendale

*"Dedicated to the members of the Llandudno Town Band,
past and present"*

"The chief function of the Band is to add to the amenities and attractions of the town, therefore the financial aspect should be regarded as of secondary importance. Even if we should end with heavy loss, this would be compensated for in the knowledge that the many thousands of visitors who stroll along the Promenade during the summer months derive no small measure of enjoyment and inspiration from the music discoursed by the Llandudno Town Band."

F. Lucio Traversi, 7th October 1940

Contents

Foreword by Gregory, Seventh Baron Mostyn

My happy engagement with the many institutions supporting the resort of Llandudno has revealed to me the wealth of voluntary commitment which the town has enjoyed over many decades. The breadth of artistic, sporting and charitable endeavour remains an important aspect of the quality of experience for both residents and visitors. This extraordinary contribution by talented and philanthropic individuals in the locality enables the resort to stay welcoming and vibrant throughout the year.

The position of the Llandudno Town Band in this regard stands high as an exemplar of how this blend of entertainment, education and civic pride can work so well. For over a century the Band has provided the quintessential promenade experience; giving sound to the spectacle. It has also supported the town in countless formal occasions and special events. In doing so, it has afforded an outlet and learning opportunity for musicians, young and old. I am delighted, therefore, that this wonderful story has now been told. The work stands, not only as a salute to the hundreds of men and women who have been part of that story, but as an important archive of local history.

I am committed, with the support of Mostyn Estates Ltd, to the development of cultural and artistic activity within Llandudno. The ambition is to offer the best of contemporary creative experience in a manner which reflects and reveals the unique traditions of the town. It is my firm hope that the Town Band remains an important part of that undertaking for many years to come.

Gregory, Seventh Baron Mostyn

Introduction

In 2008 the Llandudno Town Band was approached by the Llandudno and Colwyn Bay History Society, with a request for an evening's presentation on the history of the Band. Being the Band's drummer and thus having, in the popular mind, little to do, I was tasked with preparing an enthralling lecture.

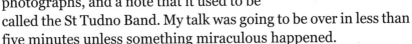

However, I was dismayed to find almost no information about the Band in any publication; just a couple of photographs, and a note that it used to be called the St Tudno Band. My talk was going to be over in less than five minutes unless something miraculous happened.

And something miraculous did happen. Mr Walter Shaw produced a large box of paperwork, salvaged from the band's first bandroom, with the words, 'You might find something in there...'

Opening that lid was my 'Howard Carter' moment; what I sought was all there, dusty, dogeared, but preserved: letters, programmes, attendance registers, balance sheets and minute books, dating from 1900; the outline of the story of a Llandudno institution.

It is not a complete record; there are books missing, attendance records haphazardly kept, and a selective collection of correspondence. But the thread of the story gleams through the spidery handwriting, and the voices of the bandsmen of long ago speak again from the yellowing pages.

Where the written records have failed, human memory must serve, and some members of the Band can remember a very long way back. Theirs is the later part of this history, incorporating many details that would not make it into a minute book, even if there was one.

It is this detail that was the impetus for writing this book. The story needed to be told, not simply about a band playing music on a bandstand, but about the Band that became an iconic part of the Llandudno scene. And, more importantly, about the men and women that made that happen.

Susan M. Wolfendale, February 2015
chatburntyas-lltbhistory@yahoo.co.uk

Acknowledgements

Compiling this collection would not have been possible without the help of a great many people, who have sought out and lent me photographs, programmes and other memorabilia. My principal thanks must go to the late Mr Walter Shaw, who rescued and cherished the box of Band archives for nearly 20 years, and to Mr George H. Brookes, who lent me an enormous box of photographs and the collection of programmes kept by Mr Traversi.

Where possible I have credited the original photographer or his company for his work, but in many cases the photographer is unknown. The photographs are reproduced with the kind permission of those who lent them to me.

Photographic credits:
Baxter's Photography; Barrow Shipyard Band; Graphic Photos, Adelphi Street; David Greenman; J. A. Jones; John and Barbara Lawson Reay; A. J. Lennie, Press Photographer; Jean Lomas; Llanrhos Studio and Post Office; Nuts and Bolts Comedy; J. G. Rowlands; Royal National Lifeboat Institution; Roj Smith; W. Symonds; Terry Taylor, Press Photographer; Peter Wareham; Llandudno Advertiser; The Daily Post and The Weekly News.

I also thank those members of the Band and their families who have spent hours exercising their memories to recall stories of the Band in times past:

Jane Bonser, George H. Brookes, Ruth Coleman Jones and the family of Walter Shaw, John J. Edwards, Lynn Emerson and the family of Robin Williams, John W. Holmes, Joan Hughes and the family of Hugh Hughes, John Hughes, Sarah Hughes,

David A. Jones, Ronald Regan of 'Nuts and Bolts'; John Ridler, Francis Traversi the younger, Cynthia Williams.

Thanks are also due to the staff at the Conwy Archive Service in Lloyd Street and at the North Wales Weekly News, and Adrian Hughes at The Home Front Museum.

My thanks to Bloodaxe Books for permission to reproduce David Constantine's poem 'The Llandudno Town Band'.

And, of course, this project would have foundered at an early stage without the constant support, encouragement, cajoling and occasional outright compulsion by my husband Clive. He and my son Richard have made this journey with me, living around piles of old papers that must not be disturbed. They have also patiently proof-read my chapters and eradicated contradictions, clumsiness and commas to allow the Band's story to shine through. My love and gratitude to them both.

Susan M. Wolfendale, February 2015

Chapter 1

Bands in Llandudno before 1910

Llandudno – 'The Queen of Welsh Resorts'

The great limestone headland of the Great Orme juts northwards into the Irish Sea, joined to the mainland only by a narrow neck of once-marshy land. St Tudno established his church high on these cliffs, and the village of Llandudno grew up nearby on the lower slopes of the Orme above the marsh. The local people mined and fished here for centuries until, in the 1840s, steamboats carrying day-trippers along the northern coast of Wales discovered the fine bathing-beaches on either side of the narrow isthmus. A local landowner, the Hon. Edward Mostyn MP (later Lord Mostyn), saw the potential in this natural asset and, together with Liverpool architect Owen Williams and surveyor George Felton, set about designing and then creating Llandudno as a seaside resort.

A Board of Improvement Commissioners, headed by Edward Mostyn's son Thomas, was established to oversee and control the development. By 1854 Mostyn Street had become the main street, soon to host some of the finest shops outside London. Hotels and hydropathic spa resorts graced the emerging promenade, one of the longest and finest in Europe. The Liverpool steamboats brought as many as 3,000 visitors a day from the newly-developing towns of Lancashire, and from 1858 the railway brought many more from the whole of Britain.

The need to provide accommodation and services for the visitors led to a dramatic increase in the resident population, and these people as well as the holidaymakers wanted their entertainments and social life. The later nineteenth century saw a growth of social, sporting and literary societies, churches of many denominations, and dance halls and theatres, such as the Pier Pavilion, the Arcadia, the Grand Theatre and the Winter Gardens. Llandudno had everything the visitor could desire – health-giving sea air, beaches and bathing, elegant shops and hotels, and entertainment in abundance; no wonder it was dubbed 'the Queen of Welsh Resorts'.

This early photograph of Llandudno shows a bandstand sited on North Parade. The 'Llandudno Town Band' of this period could have been any kind of musical ensemble, appointed annually to provide the resort's summer music programme.

The Board of Improvement Commissioners continued to keep a firm grip on the development of the town and the facilities offered to visitors. It was the Commissioners who decided what entertainment was to be allowed, particularly in the streets and on the promenade. Artistes applied annually for licences to perform in the town, and these were often revoked if the Commissioners felt the shows were unsuitable. Even the now-famous Ferrari's performing birds and Codman's 'Punch and Judy' show received regular admonishments from the authorities.

'The Llandudno Town Band'

Outdoor musical entertainment was also provided from an early date. For some years a blind harpist was licensed annually on the promenade, and in 1879 the Commissioners passed a bye-law authorising the expenditure of £100 annually for a band to perform around the town during the summer months. Although known as 'the Llandudno Town Band' this musical ensemble was not a permanent band, resident in the town. Each year the Commissioners invited any band leaders and musical directors to tender for the privilege of providing the Town Band. The successful candidate would then recruit the required number of musicians to provide daily music throughout the summer season. In order to supplement the Commissioners' £100 a collection would be taken after every concert to pay the players a living wage. Any mixture of instruments was possible; in some years the ensemble consisted of stringed instruments and piano, on other occasions the group would feature more wind instruments, and even vocalists, if

A band of musicians in Llandudno, around 1890. This photograph shows an ensemble comprising principally wind instruments, with a few strings. It is likely that Mr Underwood's band followed this pattern. (Photo: Conwy Archive Service)

approved by the Commissioners. The band leaders and players usually came from outside the town, and often worked a different seaside resort each year.

In 1894 the Board of Improvement Commissioners was replaced by the Llandudno Urban District Council, which continued to keep a firm grip on the running of the resort. The annual commissioning of the Town Band became this Council's responsibility. For several years in succession the band contract had been won by a Mr William Underwood and it became almost a formality that, having completed one summer season, he was granted the rights for the next.

Unsatisfactory Performance

However, by 1899 there were signs that the Council members were dissatisfied with the services of these musicians. In December of that year Mr Underwood was asked by the Council to engage more experienced players and provide a more varied selection of music for the next year. It was also suggested that he select his orchestra and music earlier so as to practise 'for greater efficiency', and also to consider fitting the men with uniforms.

By the next spring, 1900, Mr Underwood had arranged to obtain uniforms and 'promised to do his best to make his programmes par excellence'. The horse-drawn mobile bandstand was to be improved, with shutters and better electric lighting and a new coat of paint. After the season Mr Underwood was again granted the rights for the next year (1901) and was also allowed to play in the streets during the winter. But when the Rhyl Town and Promenade Band, under Mr De Mersy, also applied to perform in Llandudno they were allowed to play for an extended period through the winter; perhaps Mr Underwood's band was not performing 'par excellence' after all.

Mr Underwood and his band had their final chance to redeem themselves over the summer of 1901, but when the band contract came up for renewal that October, the Council decided to advertise for a new band for the 1902 season. The aforementioned De

Llandudno Town Bands in the early 1900s

Mr Mohr eventually accepted a fee of £75 for the 12 months' contract. The conditions of his employment give us some idea of the type of band working in a seaside resort at the time:

Name of Band: De Mersy's
Bandmaster: Jacob Mohr
Type of Band: Military Brass and Reed

* To provide a band of at least 16 players in the summer and 12 in the winter
* To play three days a week, Monday, Thursday and Saturday, during the winter, and every day in the summer. The Band to be absolutely under the control of the Promenade Band Sub-Committee of the Bye-Laws Committee
* To play one hour in an evening on the promenade on the Bandstand in winter
* To play in each part of the town, and at such hours, as the Committee should direct during the summer
* Summer season to begin the week before Easter 1902 until 1st October
* The Band to be allowed to collect subscriptions upon the promenade and from the houses in the streets where they play.'

The 1907 Town Band was provided by a vocalist, Mr Denbigh Cooper. Its instrumentation was more like that of a small orchestra:

'Piano
First Violin
Second violin
Viola
Double bass
Flute
Clarinet
Cornet
Trombone
Two vocalists all season, and an extra one during July.'

15

Mersy's band, who had previously worked at Southport and Rhyl, applied for the engagement. Their bandmaster, Mr Jacob Mohr, (Mr De Mersy having recently passed away) added a note to his application, asking for £150 for the year, as 'Llandudno would be far to (sic) small a place for us in the winter it would be alright in the summer season on account of the visitors being there then I know it would pay me in the summer'.

The Council favoured Mr Mohr's application but could not spend £150 on the Town Band. Instead they granted him the contract, but at a fee of £75. This was not adequate to pay a living wage for sixteen or more men for a year, so collecting subscriptions from the public was an essential activity for the bandmaster. By 1906 Mr Mohr was still providing the Llandudno Town Band, but there are signs he was struggling to make ends meet. In July the Bye-Laws Committee found it necessary to rule that the band collectors must be restricted to collecting only within a 'reasonable distance' of where the Band was playing. That September Mr Mohr announced that he could not provide a band after the end of the season.

The committee advertised for a band for the 1907 summer season. Of the five applicants, Mr Underwood was immediately eliminated – no second chance there! Eventually, Mr Denbigh Cooper, a vocalist, was contracted to provide a band from 1st May to 30th September 1907 (see panel).

Again, by the autumn of 1907, there are signs that the band situation was not satisfactory. Mr Cooper's band was not engaged for the winter, and when a Mr Groop offered to bring a band from Birkdale, Southport, the committee turned him down to give a 'local' band the opportunity to provide the town's winter music. The local St Tudno Silver Band was permitted to play two nights a week. The committee then decided not to engage a permanent summer band at all for 1908, but to spend their £100 on occasional bands. (Mr Underwood's application was turned down again...)

This photograph, part of a panorama on display at the Conwy Archives in Llandudno, shows Gloddaeth Street and bustling Edwardian crowds at the North Parade. It is believed to date from around 1906, so the military-style band in the centre, rather depleted in numbers, may therefore be the De Mersy Band, conducted by Mr Jacob Mohr. (Photo: Conwy Archive Service)

There were a number of brass bands in the Llandudno area at the end of the 19th century. This is the St Tudno Silver Band around 1896. Uniforms for the Band, including caps and music bags, were purchased from R.G. Roberts in 1893 at a total cost of £82.16s.3d. (Photo: Conwy Archive Service)

The Bright Idea

Reading between the lines, the situation was becoming desperate. This was a matter of great importance to a seaside resort – visitors expected a band on the promenade, and Llandudno did not have one worth the name. Then, in June 1908, apparently out of the blue, the Council received a letter from Mr Isaac Williams, the secretary of the aforementioned St Tudno Silver Band.

It appears that this local band was itself going through a difficult patch, being unable to find a competent bandmaster and, thus, struggling to keep the band together. The letter proposed that the Council, in effect, should take over the band: become trustee for the band's instruments, find daytime employment for a man capable of acting as bandmaster, and provide a room in which the band could practise. The band would, in return, be at the disposal of the Council for public services. It was proposed that the band should be governed by representatives of both the Council and the musicians, and would thus endeavour to become 'a credit to the town'.

Did the Council jump at the chance? Not exactly. They liked the idea of being trustees of the instruments, but deferred discussion of employing a bandmaster and providing a bandroom due to the cost implications. In the September some of the councillors urged that a local band be given the chance to entertain in the town, but caution prevailed and Mr Mohr was again engaged for the 1909 season.

Even the public were not happy with the musical situation. The Council received a petition from ratepayers, asking for two well-known bands, Royal Oakeley and Nantlle, to each be allowed to play for a week in the town. The Councillors met with Bandmaster Mohr to discuss 'what better arrangements can be made with a view to meeting the wishes of the public'.

Another year slipped by. In November 1909, when the annual contract came up for renewal, Mr Mohr's band, now conducted by Bandmaster Peter Kohl, was re-engaged for the next season. The St Tudno Band's idea was, however, still being considered, but a letter in December from their secretary makes it clear that the band was not now in a position to commit itself to fulfilling a summer season. Indeed, it had been 'lying dormant for many months, and there are a few vacancies which have to be filled.' The matter was deferred again. Plans to erect an elaborate wrought-iron bandstand, costing up to £475, on the promenade opposite Gloddaeth Crescent were also shelved; the current band (Mr Kohl's) was not worthy of the expense, and the residents and hoteliers did not like the idea of the Town Band being permanently sited outside their premises.

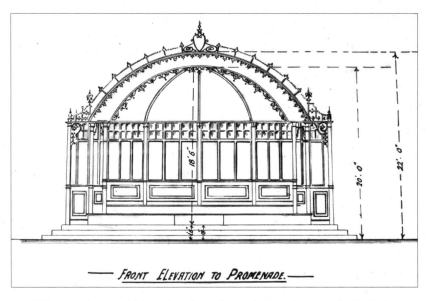

— *Front Elevation to Promenade.* —

This grand wrought-iron bandstand was designed in 1910 by E. Paley Stephenson to grace the promenade opposite Gloddaeth Crescent. Unfortunately it was never built; the musicians of the Town Band over the next century would have appreciated the shelter provided by the zinc roof and the plate glass windows on the seaward side.
(Photo: Conwy Archive Service)

The 1910 summer season got under way, with Mr Kohl's band and the old dilapidated movable platform, but their performances were unsatisfactory. The situation was obviously now urgent;

The St Tudno Silver Band around 1908-1910. By their own admission, the Band was 'dormant', with only 23 players shown in this photograph and no apparent bandmaster.
Left to right, back row: Ivor Evans, Edward Roberts, James Williams, Arthur Evans, Harold Olive, W. Hughes, Jack 'Salem' Edwards, J. Edwards and Walter Maitland;
Second row: R. Lunt, H. Edwards, J.I. Roberts, R. Williams, John Roberts, W. Lloyd, W. Hughes:
Front row: Samuel Edwards, W.J. Jones, Arthur Edwards, H. Jones, Ll. Evans, Isaac Williams and Robert Edwards.
(Photo: North Wales Weekly News)

remarks at a Council meeting, perhaps tongue-in-cheek, refer to the current promenade band having 'five people playing and seven collecting'! Thus on 2nd June 1910 the Clerk to the Council was instructed to re-open negotiations with the St Tudno Band, and on this occasion no time was wasted.

On 2nd July 1910 the full Council approved an agreement with the St Tudno Band, exactly as proposed two years before. The Trust Deed, formally sealed on 22nd July, was signed by Arthur Edwards, Samuel Edwards and Isaac Williams on behalf of the Band, and by Ernest Edgar Bone on behalf of the Council.

Llandudno had its own Town Band at last.

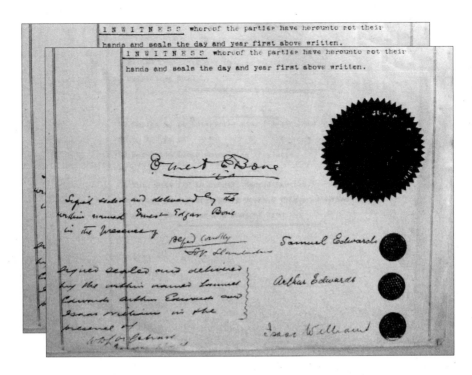

Signatures on the formal indenture document of 1910 by which the St Tudno Silver Band became the permanent Llandudno Town Band.

Chapter 2

Establishing the New Band, 1910-1914

A Bandroom and a Bandmaster

After the inordinate length of time taken by the Council to make their momentous decision, the pace of subsequent developments must have seemed like a whirlwind to the members of the former St Tudno Band. By 8th August the advertisements for the position of bandmaster had been posted. A room above the fire station on Market Street, behind the Council Yard and Town Hall, was allocated to the Band as a practice-room. A band committee was formed, with representatives from the Urban District Council and the Band (see panel).

The first task of this committee was to appoint a bandmaster from the thirty-six applications received by mid-August. They reported some difficulty in selecting a suitable candidate, having regard to essential qualifications and the salaries requested by the applicants. Eventually, the Committee decided to invite a Mr F. Lucio Traversi of Barrow in Furness for an interview and audition on the evening of 15th August.

'Mr Traversi satisfactorily answered all questions put to him and afterwards conducted to the satisfaction of the Committee the performance by the Members of the Band of one or two pieces of Music.'

Mr Traversi was offered the post and took up the appointment on 1st October 1910. And so began the career of one of Llandudno's unsung heroes, a man who, through his passion and dedication, would contribute so much to the fame and prosperity of the resort.

The Band Committee 1910-11

Councillor Pierce Jones Penrhyn Crescent
(Chairman)

Representing the Band:

John Roberts	13 Madoc Street
Isaac Williams	Hazlemere, Maelgwyn Terrace
Arthur Edwards	12 Madoc Street
Samuel Edwards	2 Eden Cottages
Walter Maitland	The Dingle, Bodhyfryd Road

Representing the Urban District Council:

Thomas Jones	10 Tudno Street
R. Jones	York Villa, Clifton Road
John Roberts	Bryn Celyn, Abbey Road
R. Roberts J.P.	50 Madyn Street
F.J. Sarson	County Chambers, Mostyn Street
J.J. Marks	Abbey Road
Ernest Edgar Bone	Llewelyn Chambers
J. Vaughan Humphreys	Maenan House, Lloyd Street
W. Wood (Treasurer)	

Mr F. L. Traversi

Francis Lucio Traversi was born on 21st November 1873 in the gold-mining town of Ross, on the Totara River on the South Island of New Zealand. He was one of (at least) three children of Antonio and Susan Traversi. It is thought that Antonio's parents migrated from northern Italy at the time of the New Zealand 'gold rush' in the mid-nineteenth century. Although he grew up in a bushland environment with apparently few educational opportunities, Francis read widely and was very articulate and literate. He could quote freely from the classics and often had an appropriate quotation to hand. He learned the cornet and the violin, and early in life conceived a passion for brass bands. It became his ambition to travel to Great Britain, the home of the great brass band competitions at Belle Vue, Manchester, and Crystal Palace, London.

By 1901 he had arrived in England. He set about attending all the brass band competitions he could, and, by talking with the musicians and commenting on their band's performances, he soon gained a reputation as an astute unofficial adjudicator. He also impressed with his cornet playing, winning several cornet solo competitions. This resulted in his receiving a number of letters from all over the country offering him band conductorships, for at this time a conductor often played the principal cornet part as well as directing the ensemble. He chose to go to the Barrow Shipyard Band at Barrow in Furness.

Francis threw all his energies into building up the Barrow Band and by 1906 the new smart uniforms and improved musicianship had made it an important part of the ceremonial of the launching of new ships at the shipyard. In 1908 it was given official backing by the Vickers company and was renamed the Barrow Shipyard Prize Band. Mr Traversi's dedication even allegedly went as far as buying essential instruments out of his own meagre savings. Unfortunately, he later found that the band secretary had been exaggerating the parlous state of the Band's finances, and had in fact been 'diverting' the money! It was this uncomfortable situation which prompted Francis to apply for the bandmaster's post at Llandudno.

Francis Lucio Traversi (front row, centre) was appointed bandmaster of the Barrow Shipyard Band around 1901. The bandmaster was expected to supplement the solo cornet section as well as direct the performance. In this 1901 photograph the Band is seated in front of the General Offices of shipbuilders Vickers Sons and Maxim Ltd. (Photo: Barrow Shipyard Band)

Settling in at Llandudno

The Band contract stipulated that the Llandudno Council would provide a daytime post for the bandmaster, and Mr Traversi's initial employment was to assist in tidying up the Lending Library until something permanent could be found. It was then proposed that he be a market supervisor, but in late October he became an electricity meter reader. In addition to his salary he would be paid £39 a year for his bandmaster's duties.

What had Mr Traversi taken on? By their own admission the erstwhile St Tudno Band was 'dormant', without a full complement of players and having had no regular bandmaster for some time. They possessed a full set of instruments but a fairly limited selection of music. There was also the question of uniforms and a bandstand. It would be quite a challenge for the new bandmaster.

Let us consider for a moment: the Council's band budget was £100; the bandmaster's salary would take £39; this would leave only £61 towards the Band's expenses for the whole year, which would include paying the players each time they performed. In addition, the town's mobile bandstand was in a very poor state of repair after being well used for performances over several years. It is clear the Councillors were uneasy about the financial side of their new venture; they even turned down Mr Traversi's first request for £5 to buy music, and applied instead to the Evening Classes Fund for a grant 'towards the expense of providing tuition for the Band'. After all, they didn't know whether there would actually be a viable band for the next season.

However, Mr Traversi settled down to his task straight away, beginning a learners' class and recruiting new members to bring the senior band up to strength. On 13th January 1911, just three months after taking up the post, he presented his first Bandmaster's Report to the Committee, which indicated his satisfaction with progress to date and expressed his optimism for the future (see panel).

The Band Committee presented this report and a very positive set of suggestions to the full Council meeting of 9th March 1911. It was proposed that the new Band would play for three nights each week from Whitsuntide until the end of September. 'In their enthusiasm the (bands)men were prepared to accept a nominal payment for their services' – one shilling and sixpence 1s 6d. each man, making a total cost for the season of £95. 12s. The £61 balance of the Council grant would partly cover this, and would be supplemented by charging the audience for chairs, and by taking a collection at each concert. There was even a possibility that more funds would be available, subject to approval from the Local Government Board, if the Band also performed periodically in the Happy Valley Recreation Grounds. The Band Committee members were sure that, with the co-operation of the Council, (which meant providing music stands, uniforms and a bandstand), the Promenade Concerts would be a 'permanent additional attraction to the Town'.

Their representation worked; Mr Traversi's initial successes persuaded the Council they were backing a winner. £45 was provided as a loan towards uniforms, and a new bandstand on wheels was hurriedly constructed in time for the summer season.

Mr Traversi's first report to the Committee, 13th January 1911

"GENTLEMEN,

As it is now some three months since I took up my appointment as Conductor of your Band, I beg to submit a brief report on matters appertaining to my charge.

I am very pleased to inform you the progress made by the Band, from a musical standpoint, has quite exceeded my most sanguine expectation.

Consequent upon the learners' class having progressed, I have now promoted the members to the ranks of the Band, the total strength of which is now 27, not including two drummers and myself. The instruments are all taken up.

I have found the members very diligent, and anxious to strive in every way for the welfare of the Band.

During the past two months 18 parades have been made, viz: General parades through the Town, 6; Charity, 4; Christmas and New Year, 9, and one Funeral.

Regarding the proposed performances on the Promenade. If it is desired that the Band should play in the evenings during the season, I am prepared to undertake that it will be fully efficient, provided due notice be given me.

In conclusion, I desire to say I have no doubt, given favourable circumstances – steady employment to members and a continuance of their present enthusiasm – the progress will be even more rapid in the near future than hitherto.

I am,
Your obedient Servant,
F. LUCIO TRAVERSI
Bandmaster."

The First Summer Season 1911

By June 1911 things were going so well the Band decided to play every evening (except Sundays) either on the promenade or in the Happy Valley. This led to complaints of the frequency of concerts outside some premises on the Parade! They were allowed the free use of the Assembly Rooms in the Town Hall if the weather was wet. The Band also undertook to be available for civic functions on George V's Coronation Day 22nd June and The Prince of Wales' Investiture Day 13th July – which latter day incidentally saw the old bandstand consigned to the celebratory bonfire!

The new Llandudno Town Band at the Pier Pavilion. This photograph was taken in Coronation Year 1911, to celebrate the arrival of their new uniforms; several of the players are recognisable from the earlier St Tudno Band photograph, but Mr Traversi (centre, in cap, still sporting his neat moustache) has apparently not yet obtained his bandmaster's frock coat.
(Photo: W. Symonds)

At the end of the summer season the Band showed a healthy profit. Some of this was repaid to the Council and the rest was divided amongst the players as a bonus. Mr Traversi was allowed the proceeds of a benefit concert as his bonus. The Band Committee asked the Council to increase his allowance for the next season, and eventuallyhe was allowed £2 10s per week, but with no benefit concert! Instead he was paid 10% commission on advertisements in the programmes.

The bandstand saga rumbled on. The temporary platform made for the 1911 season, nicknamed 'the Juggernaut', was declared 'inadequate' by Mr Traversi, and eventually in January 1912 the Council resolved to build a movable bandstand, not heavier than 2 tons, and to spread the not-inconsiderable cost of £205 over five years. They must have felt by now that the Band was worth it. However, there was some delay in providing this...

A photograph of East Parade, Llandudno, showing the 'Juggernaut' on the promenade on the right. This bandstand was built as a temporary measure in 1911, and had to be repaired many times before a permanent bandstand was provided.

Building on Early Success

By late 1911, Mr Traversi had coached the Band to such proficiency that he obtained the Council's permission to enter the Band into the Colwyn Bay band contest on New Year's Day 1912, although they did not win a prize. During the winter and spring of 1912 Mr

Traversi kept the Band in trim by participating in a series of monthly concerts at the Town Hall. The programmes featured local singers and choirs as well as the Band, which typically only performed three or four pieces during the evening. Mr Traversi had by this time evidently been able to spend money on music, as the early programmes feature selections such as 'The Mikado', 'The Pirates of Penzance', the overture 'Raymond', and a descriptive fantasia called 'A Military Church Parade'.

Over the years Mr Traversi kept copies of many of the Band's concert programmes, and these are still in the Band's possession. The programmes for the summer seasons show the increasing amount of music in the Band's library. Even in 1912 the list of pieces in the repertoire ran to 126; 28 marches, 14 waltzes, 13 quick-steps, 5 overtures, 31 selections and fantasias, 6 American

LLANDUDNO TOWN BAND.

This photograph appeared on the programme brochure for the 1912 summer season of promenade concerts in Llandudno. The brochure contained a list of the pieces in the Band's repertoire, so the audience could identify the pieces being played during the concert. Over the next twenty years the lists in the summer brochures grew ever longer and the music more varied, as Mr Traversi kept the Band's library up to date.

marches and cake-walks, and 26 miscellaneous items, most of them instrumental solos. When playing on the promenade, the number of the piece being played was displayed on the bandstand so that the audience could find its title in the programme index – this encouraged them to buy a programme, of course!

A Hard Taskmaster

This may be a good point to pause and consider one of the most remarkable and surprising things about Mr Francis Lucio Traversi: he was virtually deaf. Such a condition was a great handicap in those days; without hearing aids and sympathetic social attitudes it was much harder to get on in life. Mr Traversi had found that there was no hope of advancement working for an employer; the deaf would always be overlooked when it came to promotion. For this reason the post of bandmaster suited him admirably, as he was the man in charge.

He was very strict, and, as any discussion or argument with him was difficult because of his deafness, this may have led to frustrations and dissatisfactions. Mr Traversi seems to have inspired the loyalty and dedication of many Band members over the years, but there must have been some who did not like either his style or the commitment he demanded of them. He was uncompromising in his efforts to improve his Band. For example, bandsmen were fined 3d if they were not ready on time for concerts. A Mr W. J. Jones was dismissed from the Band for taking on an evening employment, which meant he could not attend the summer concerts, nor rehearsals in winter. Others were dismissed if they missed too many engagements or practices. The bandmaster considered a Mr J. E. Edwards 'inefficient' as a player, and as a result Mr Edwards absented himself from concerts and rehearsals. After appearing before the Committee he was given a chance to continue as a member, providing he obtained eye-glasses within seven days! Perhaps poor sight was the reason he was 'inefficient'. He did not respond to this olive-branch, however, and was dismissed.

But the majority of the bandsmen were very keen and, although most worked full-time during the day, gave their spare time willingly in support of the Band's many engagements. They also turned out on occasions for charitable causes or benefit concerts. One such was arranged by the Celts Football Club in aid of a Mr Joe Taylor, who had been laid up in the Cottage Hospital for some considerable time, with a consequent loss of income for his family. Another was in aid of the Deganwy Brotherhood Choir. The Band members also went to the trouble of painting a special banner and parading through the town in May 1912 to raise funds for the Titanic Disaster Fund. They collected £9.5s.2d and were accorded a 'hearty vote of thanks' by the Band Committee.

Musical and Financial Success 1912-13

In October 1912 Mr Traversi was able to report that the Band had made 97 public appearances that summer, 69 of them on the promenade. Unfortunately several concerts had had to be abandoned because of rain – the proposed £205 bandstand had not yet materialised, and again there was a plea for a structure with shelter over it, to prevent damage to music and uniforms. Even so, the profit at the end of the season was £59.10s.10d. Half of this was handed over to the Council to purchase more deck-chairs for the following year, as audiences were already growing beyond the existing capacity.

During the 1913 season, the 'Juggernaut' was very busy, trundling noisily about each day – on Mondays, it was sited on the promenade opposite St George's Crescent; on Tuesdays, opposite Gloddaeth Crescent; on Wednesday there were two separate performances, at Craig y Don and opposite Mostyn Crescent; on Thursdays, in the Happy Valley; on Fridays, on the West Shore and St George's Crescent; and on Saturdays, back to the Happy Valley. It was decided the Band should not play on Sundays.

At this time the secretary of the Band was a Mr W. D. Longshaw. In September 1913 it was found that certain monies had disappeared from the Band's account. Mr Longshaw may also

The Disaster at the Universal Colliery, Senghenydd

The village of Senghenydd, near Caerffili in Glamorgan, owes its existence to the rich seams of coal which were discovered there during the 1890s. The Universal Colliery was established by the Universal Steam Coal Company and became one of the deepest mines of the South Wales coalfield. By 1913 some of the workfaces were two miles from the pit-shafts in the village, and the mine had a reputation for being hot, dry and liable to gas. Up to a thousand men could be in the mine at any one time.

The mine had suffered a disastrous explosion in 1901, in which 82 men died underground. As a result of the subsequent investigation several safety recommendations were made, but even by 1913 some of these had still not been implemented.

On the morning of October 14th 1913 the day shift had been down in the workings for two hours when several underground explosions ripped through the levels. The cage and gear of one of the two shafts was wrecked and could not be used to assist in the rescue attempts. As the day wore on it was found that the East side of the mine was not affected, and the men there were gradually brought to the surface, but those in the West side were cut off by roof-falls and the fires raging along the levels.

The final death-toll reached 439, many of whose bodies were never recovered. It remains the worst mining disaster in the history of the British coalfields.

have administered other Council funds as the Band minutes refer to 'the Council's pending claim on the insurance company'. Mr Longshaw was dismissed as secretary, and Mr Traversi took on the role for the rest of the season. The Band's deficiency due to this incident amounted to £18.17s.5d; this may not sound a great deal of money to us nowadays, but if we consider that subsequently Town Hall clerks were invited to apply for the post of secretary of the Band at an allowance of £6.6s per annum, we realise that the secretary was actually handling temptingly large amounts of money.

The series of winter concerts began on 8th November 1913 and again the Band, with their fellow artists, turned out to help others in distress. The proceeds of this first concert were donated to the Senghenydd Disaster Fund, only three weeks after that terrible event had occurred (see panel). The programme featured a soprano cornet solo, 'Will Ye No Come Back Again?' played by Master R.O. Williams. Young 'Reggie' joined the learners' Band in 1912 and went on to be one of the Band's longest-serving members. There were also songs by local artists and a duet on Musical Glasses.

The fortnightly concerts continued through to 21st March, and it is noticeable that Mr Traversi was providing some of his star pupils with a chance to perform in public. During that winter, cornet solos were played not only by Master Reggie Williams but also by Master Robbin Williams and Master Robert Edwards. This was to prove a fortunate policy.

Chapter 3

The Great War 1914-1918

By the spring of 1914 the pattern of Band activity had been established, and the Band Committee was increasingly leaving decisions in the hands of the bandmaster. The Band had proved its worth and was trusted to get on with the job. The Band Committee met less frequently and was mostly concerned with payments to players and purchase of equipment, rather than keeping a firm grip on the day-to-day organisation of engagements. An important priority was to pin down the town surveyor regarding estimates for the bandstand proposed in 1912, which had evidently been quietly forgotten as long as the 'temporary' platform was still working. But in his 1913 report Mr Traversi had recorded, 'I may add that almost every evening during the season visitors addressed to me remarks of disapproval of the structure which now serves as a bandstand', so perhaps this time their application would be successful?

The Outbreak of War

But events in 1914, of course, took a turn for the worse, and it was by no means certain that there would be a need for a bandstand at all. Strangely, the outbreak of the Great War on 4th August 1914 is not mentioned in the minutes of the Band Committee, but it appears from the Band register that some of the bandsmen hardly waited for the season to finish before enlisting to fight. At that time the Welsh regiments were recruiting large numbers, and many were quartered in the Llandudno area. On 10th November 1914 the minutes record:

'The Bandmaster reported that some of the bandsmen had joined Lord Kitchener's army. The Committee felt very sorry to lose their services and hoped they would soon return'.

Like the Pied Piper, the Band (with Mr Traversi in front of the tram) leads the townsfolk in a recruitment parade in September 1914 along Mostyn Street, Llandudno. The Band never wore their uniforms for these parades, perhaps to show civilian support for the war effort. Ironically, the call to arms was heeded by several members of the Band itself, and even at this early date there are already a number of boys filling positions in the formation.

Mr Traversi went on to relate that the Band had already held a concert in aid of the local War Relief Fund, and another was proposed in aid of the Refugee Fund, for which the usual admission fees would be doubled. The players turned out in their own time on 2nd December to meet the first detachment of the 'London Welsh' at the railway station, and marched them to North Parade, as a welcome from the town.

But in 1915, by and large, life went on as normal; in spite of the war visitors still came to Llandudno and the town's entertainments needed to continue in order to maintain the town's prosperity. But the Band was short of players; seven members had enlisted in the army, namely:

Robert John Davies	solo horn
John Edwards	principal solo cornet
Peter Price	Eb bass
John Richards	2nd horn
William Henry Tyrer	bass, euphonium
Robert Williams	Eb bass
Reggie O. Williams	soprano cornet

Two others, J. Martin, Eb bass, and Llewelyn Evans (Ettrick Villa), 2nd trombone, who worked at the gas works and the electricity works respectively, were working permanent night shifts and were unable to attend the Band. With the loss of so many players the Band simply would not be able to operate.

The Boys Save the Day
The Band was saved by the young boys of the learners' band. By this time some of the boys in Mr Traversi's training group were becoming proficient enough to be considered for the 'senior combination', and now the situation demanded that they be thrown in at the deep end. Mr Traversi was tireless in his efforts to bring these players up to the required standard; they were not be allowed to hold back the Band's performance. They themselves rose to the challenge magnificently; after two wartime summer seasons Mr Traversi was able to report:

'Before the season commenced some doubt was expressed as to the ability of the Band to maintain efficiency consistent with the task before it. This impression arose in consequence of the inclusion of young lads whom I had trained to fill the places of men serving with the Colours. I will now say without hesitation that from a musical point the Band in the 1916 season was

37

The Llandudno Town Band continued to provide entertainment in the town throughout the First World War. This was only possible because boys from the learners' band were drafted in to replace men who had joined the army. The standard of the boys' playing attracted admiration even in the national press. In this photograph, printed on the 1916 summer programme, more than half of the players are under sixteen years of age.

better than ever, and the programmes given would compare with any of those of the best British contesting bands, if put to test of giving nightly performances for several months in succession. I desire to record my appreciation of the loyalty and excellent spirit shown by the bandsmen in the interest of the Band, indeed I feel honoured to have such a hardworking and self-sacrificing body of players under my charge.'

Llandudno Town Band was one of the very few bands who managed to keep going throughout the war, using only local players, notably several Williams', Jones', Evans', Davies', Roberts' and Hughes'. Most other resorts lost their local bands to enlistments and only maintained their entertainments by means of bands of foreign musicians.

Musicians in Wartime

By this time the former De Mersy's Band had become the Colwyn Bay Town Band. You will remember their former bandmasters, Mr Jacob Mohr and Mr Peter Kohl; it would appear that this Band relied on a number of other players of middle European origin who had settled in the town. In the autumn of 1914 the 'British Bandsman' newspaper notes that the Colwyn Bay Town Band had been 'hooted by excursionists' in a show of anti-German patriotism. Later in the war, musicians Harry Degau, Jacob Baumber, Jacob Langwasser and Emil Ulrich were interned as potentially dangerous aliens, and their destitute families were accorded Poor Relief by the Colwyn Bay Town Council.

As the war continued, more of the Llandudno players enlisted:

Humphrey Davies	repiano cornet
Sidney A. Edwards	flugel horn
Llewelyn Evans (Chapel St)	Eb bass
William Foulkes	1st horn
Richard Hughes	baritone
Robert T. Jones	solo cornet
J. E. Edwards	cornet
J. W. Edwards	cornet
Ivor Evans	cornet
R. Owen	cornet
Isaac Williams	Bb bass

Some also returned; Reggie Williams, having left in late 1914, was back for the 1915 and 1916 summer seasons, but was absent again throughout 1917 and 1918. Llewelyn Evans (Chapel St) is later recorded as 'returned' but apparently did not play with the Band again.

There are few detailed records about the Band's activities during the war years. It appears the winter concert series may have been suspended, as there are no programmes in the collection between March 1915 and November 1919. The summer concerts

A funeral procession led by the Band passes the Town Hall, the coffin draped with a Union flag. During the Great War the Band provided this patriotic service free of charge, but later, as military funerals continued into the 1920s, they began to charge a fee for their attendance.

continued as normal on the promenade and around the town. One innovation of wartime, which we take for granted now, was the Daylight Saving Act of 1916, or 'putting the clocks forward'. Intended to save power in a time of shortages, the additional hour of daylight enabled the Band to continue its season well into September, whereas in 1915 they had had to stop on 27th August as electricity could not be spared to light the bandstand. The Band was so popular that, in spite of several additional purchases of deck-chairs, the seating accommodation was 'taxed to its utmost' and financial returns were as high as ever.

The tragedies of war were never far away, and funding-raising events for the war effort, refugees and other victims of the conflict were a regular part of the Band's activities. On 5th August 1917

Lord Roberts Memorial Workshops for Disabled Soldiers and Sailors

Field Marshal Frederick Sleigh Roberts, 1st Earl Roberts VC KG KP GCB OM GCSI GCIE KStJ VD PC, of Kandahar, Pretoria, and Waterford, was the most successful soldier of the Victorian era, a much-decorated hero of the Second Afghan War and South African War, and commander in chief of the army 1901-1904. He had long campaigned for more to be done to help retired servicemen, and he took a keen interest in the workshops for disabled veterans which had been founded in the late 1890s by the Countess of Meath.

After his death in 1914 the Workshops were renamed in his memory and expanded until there were eleven around the country. The Band first established an association with the Memorial Fund in 1917, and this continued for several years, an August benefit concert still being performed in 1938. The Lord Roberts Fund is now amalgamated with the SSAFA organisation.

'The public, for whom so many of our soldiers and sailors have been injured in war and disabled from following their former avocations, should do all in their power to support the Lord Roberts Memorial Scheme; it helps these brave men to help themselves, and it is little enough we can do to redeem our debt.'

(*British Journal of Nursing*, 30 Jun 1917)

began a long-running association with the Lord Roberts Memorial Workshops for Disabled Soldiers and Sailors (see panel).

The End of the War

Hostilities eventually ceased on 11th November 1918 but, unfortunately, not soon enough for cornet and flugel player Sidney Albert Edwards. The son of Samuel (bass player) and E. L. Edwards of Cwlach Road, Llandudno, he was a Lance-Corporal in the 17th Battalion Royal Welsh Fusiliers. He was killed in action in the Cambrai area of northern France on 29th October 1918, aged 21. He is buried in Englefontaine British Cemetery, not far from the Belgian border, and is commemorated on the Llandudno War Memorial on the promenade.

After the war the town of Llandudno was presented with a tank from the front line as a memorial. A grainy silent film entitled 'Llandudno receives a tank – A peaceful end' shows the Band, with Mr Traversi in his customary position at the rear right, leading the battle-scarred tank no. 27 along the street. The film is, at the time of writing, available to view on the British Pathe website (britishpathe.com).

By the time of Mr Traversi's report of 15th April 1919 nine of the enlisted bandsmen had been demobilised from the army and had rejoined the Band. These were: J. Edwards, Ivor Evans, R.J. Davies, R. Hughes, R.O. Williams, Peter Price, J.E. Edwards, W. Tyrer, and E.R. Roberts. Other players may also have returned but injuries may have prevented them playing instruments again. It is known that Peter Price experienced a gas attack in the trenches and suffered respiratory problems all his life – perhaps playing a tuba thereafter was actually beneficial to his health. Mr Traversi concluded, with evident satisfaction, that 'From a musical point of view the prospects of the Band are particularly bright, and there is now no doubt, this year the Town will have at its command a band of its own never before equalled, and [it] will I am sure rank as a first-rate attraction to Llandudno'.

Dated '1919', this photograph may show the Band embarking on a social event. Mr Traversi is immediately above the standing gentleman, in a dark coat and hat, with his son Tony on his knee. To the right of him are two gentlemen with moustaches, Bill Lloyd and Dick Hughes.

Chapter 4

Moving On – the 1920s

Personnel and equipment

By 1920 most of the upheaval of the war years had subsided and the Band was in a position to rebuild and develop. Mr Traversi records the 1920 season as the most successful in the band's history to date, both in the number of engagements and the financial returns. In addition to the promenade concerts, the Band undertook a large number of parades in connection with public functions, unfortunately 'mostly military funerals'. The winter concert season was taken up again, with fortnightly concerts from November through to April.

Over the next few seasons there was almost a full complement of players; the standard instrumentation of a brass band is 25 players plus a percussion section, which may vary in its requirements according to the music being performed (see panel).

Instrumentation of a Brass Band

Brass band music is arranged in such a way that within the band there are several sub-sections of instruments, forming individual 'choirs' within the whole. For example, the three tenor horns each have a separate line of music written for them, so when they play together they produce the sound of a chord. Some instruments have their own individual part to play, others play the same notes as the instrument next to them.

A 'full complement' is therefore:

High pitched instruments:
1 x soprano cornet – a very high-pitched cornet accentuating the high notes.

4 x solo cornets – the most difficult cornet parts, usually playing the melody and difficult ornamentations. All four play the same notes, giving a strong sound, but with the Principal taking solo passages.

1 x repiano cornet – sometimes plays the same as the solo cornets, but often has a quite independent part.

2 x 2nd cornets – both playing the same notes, usually less difficult and lower pitched than solo cornet parts.

2 x 3rd cornets – both playing the same notes, usually lower pitched and often less difficult than 2nd cornet parts.

1 x flugel horn – sometimes the same as repiano cornet, but often with its own solo passages.

Medium pitched instruments:

1 x solo tenor horn – the highest horn part, with solo passages.

1 x 1st tenor horn – the middle horn part.

1 x 2nd tenor horn – the lowest horn part, usually less difficult.

Medium to low pitched instruments:

1 x 1st baritone – a fairly difficult part, sometimes with solo passages.

1 x 2nd baritone – usually not as difficult as the 1st baritone part.

2 x euphoniums - both playing the same part, but with the Principal taking solo passages.

1 x 1st trombone – the highest trombone part, with solo passages.

1 x 2nd trombone – the middle trombone part.

1 x bass trombone – the lowest trombone part, often playing the same as the basses.

Low pitched instruments:

2 x E flat (Eb) basses (tubas) – the smaller tubas, playing the bass part of the music.

2 x B flat (Bb) basses – playing the same as the Eb basses, but being larger instruments they can be used to achieve even deeper notes.

Percussion – drum kit, timpani, glockenspiel, xylophone, cymbals, tambourine, triangle, etc.

During the first few seasons of the 1920s the personnel notes printed in the programmes for the summer seasons indicate that the Band had a few vacancies, usually lacking a second euphonium and two or three cornets. But as these instruments play 'strengthening' roles in an orchestration their absence would have made little difference to the sound of the Band; the other cornets and euphonium would just have had to work a bit harder, and would not have been able to take a rest now and then! It is also likely that juniors were allowed to play on occasions to make up the numbers, and thus would not appear on the printed lists.

In May 1924 one of the original St Tudno signatories of the Band's Trust Deed, Arthur Edwards decided to retire, and in March the year after, long-serving cornettist J. Edwards wrote that he could not 'tackle another season of promenade playing'.

Shortages of players were often covered by other players changing instruments. One feature of a brass band, as opposed to a military band or orchestra, is the facility of players to change from one instrument to another. All of the valved brass instruments are played using the same fingering system, so a player does not have to learn a different technique when he changes instrument. This meant that the full line-up could be maintained even though players left the band. The personnel lists in the summer programmes show that Robin H. Williams, for example, who joined the Band as a youngster on tenor horn during the war, played the 1924 and 1925 seasons on soprano cornet in the absence of R. J. Edwards, but when a new soprano player arrived in 1926 Robin moved on to solo euphonium. The aforementioned Reggie Williams was the principal solo cornet for many years before moving on to solo trombone.

A more serious problem was the absence for many years of a regular drummer. In 1927 a Mr Joseph Baxter was hired to play in a town hall concert, and he came all the way from Tyldesley, Manchester. The Band wanted him to be their permanent drummer, but local employment apparently could not be found for him. The situation still had not been resolved the next year, as

Mr Traversi appealed to the Council on 17th May 1928 to find daytime employment for any suitable percussion player. It was not until the 1929 season that a drummer, Mr Owen Williams, was named on the summer programme. He was evidently a multi-talented percussionist, as he is recorded in the programme of 1st September 1929 as the soloist in a xylophone solo, 'Sparks'.

New Instruments

By 1920, the Band's instruments had been in use almost every evening for at least ten years – we do not know how long the St

The Llandudno Town Band, pictured around 1921, displaying their first items of silverware. The players, as recorded on the reverse of this photograph, are: Back row, left to right: Ivor Parry, Ivor Evans, John Llew Jones, Jack Edwards (Salem), R. O. (Reg) Williams, Bill Killen, Bobby Edwards, Harry Williams, Ben Johns (Orme), Roger Killen. Second row: Dick Hughes, Jack Martin, Mr Edwards (plumber), F.L.Traversi (Bandmaster), Robin Williams, John Hughes, Tommy Wynn. Front row, seated: Llew Evans (Mim Evans' brother), Mr Williams (coal), Elyn Roberts, Robert John Davies, Tommy Hughes (landau and horses, Jubilee St), B. Evans, Peter Price, Bill Lloyd (plumber). Front row, small boys: Bill Evans, Robin Williams (Ty-Isa)

Tudno Band had had them before 1910 – and this heavy usage was taking its toll. Brass instruments can last for very many years but their moving parts become less efficient through wear, and they inevitably suffer damage and dents which can affect their tuning. In May 1920 a complete new set of 'Enharmonics' was purchased from the famous Besson company of London, the old set being sold to a Mr Newbold. The players were reported to be delighted with the sound of the new instruments.

However, in the early 1920s various instrument makers were experimenting to improve both the tone and tuning of brass instruments, particularly the basses (tubas). Besson developed the 'New Standard' model, Boosey and Co. produced the 'Imperial Compensator' and Hawkes and Son made the new 'Profundo' model. When the Band was looking to update their set of basses in March 1925, several instruments were sent on trial from all three manufacturers, and the choice eventually fell to the Boosey Imperials.

Contests
In the early years of the 1920s Mr Traversi was evidently satisfied that the Band had achieved a sufficiently high standard to enter competitions without disgracing either itself or the town. The first indication of success is printed on the 1922 summer programme:

'Winners 5 First Prizes and 2 Cups in 1921. Soloists awarded 6 First Prize Medals in 1921'.

From then on, the tally increases annually:

1922: Winners 9 First Prizes 1921-1922, including Anglesey Chair Eisteddfod Challenge Cup twice in succession
1923: Winners 12 First Prizes 1921-1922-1923, including Anglesey Chair Eisteddfod Challenge Cup three times in succession

A new permanent bandstand was constructed during 1925-26 by engineer W. T. Ward and builder David Williams of Builder Street. The bandsmen objected at the time to it having a concrete floor, but the construction had to be sturdy enough to withstand the onshore weather as well as the weight of the superstructure. (Photos: J. G. Rowlands)

1924: Winners 17 First Prizes 1921-1924, including Anglesey Chair Eisteddfod Challenge Cup three times in succession
1925: Winners of 19 First Prizes since 1921
1926: Winners of 20 First Prizes since 1921
1927: Winners of 21 First Prizes since 1921

In 1923 the Band was 'selected to compete at the Belle Vue (Manchester) contest on 5th May', and special concerts were arranged to raise money 'for the Fund to Defray the Band's expenses' for this event. The contest was won by Denton Original Band, Llandudno were unplaced. After 1927 the run of success seems to dry up, and in 1930 the style of programme brochure was changed, with no mention of contest prizes. Since that era the Band has only contested sporadically, although occasionally with success.

The Bandstand
In 1924 the old 'Juggernaut' bandstand, having been dragged about continually for 14 seasons, was getting shabby and attracting derogatory remarks from Llandudno's visitors (according to Mr Traversi). The Council Joiner was of the opinion that it was useless trying to repair it yet again, so at last the Council decided to build a permanent bandstand on the promenade. The location chosen was in front of the Imperial Hotel on Gloddaeth Crescent. In the event, the poor 'Juggernaut' had to survive for two more seasons before the new bandstand was ready. It was eagerly anticipated by the bandsmen until they learned, at the eleventh hour, that it was to have a concrete floor. They complained that this would be 'fatal to the Band as it was almost impossible to play on a concrete floor' (minutes, 27th April 1926) – the reason is not given, but was presumably due to the lack of resonance of the material.

The Band Committee was asked to make representations to the Council for a wooden floor, and improved lighting. It was also a disappointment that there was to be no cover over the bandstand to protect against rain and to help the projection of the sound.

The Promenade Bandstand opposite the Imperial Hotel was inaugurated on Whit Monday 1926. Canvas screens were added for the following season to protect the players from the cold sea winds.
Back row, left to right: cornets Ivor Parry, T.G.Brookes?, Tony Traversi?, Ben Jones?; basses T. Ward, Peter Price, T.A. Wynne, Isaac Williams; trombones W. Evans, R.J. Davies, H. Edwards.
Front row, seated, left to right: cornets Reg Williams, W. Killen, John Ll. Jones, unknown; tenor horns E.R. Roberts, J. Hughes, Bandmaster F.L. Traversi, R. Holland; baritones R. Hughes, Ivor Evans; euphoniums T.G. Holland, Robin H. Williams.

However, the design was not changed, and the new bandstand was inaugurated on Whit Monday 1926. Mr Traversi reported later that several concerts that summer had to be curtailed due to cold winds blowing in from the sea – he requested the bandstand be provided with shelter screens for the next year. The first photograph of the new bandstand appears on the 1928 summer brochure.

Promenade Concerts

The band's concerts were always very popular with the holiday crowds, attracting audiences of several hundreds for most performances. The young learners had to serve their time as deck-chair assistants and money-collectors before they could play with the main Band. Collecting money was still very important as the Band paid the players not only for each performance, but also for any loss of earnings incurred through daytime engagements, and then a bonus at the end of the season. There was at one time a suggestion that the Council might take over as the actual employer of the Band instead of it being run as a self-supporting voluntary organization. But it was discovered that this would entail the players having to join the Musicians' Union, with a guaranteed wage for them and the deck-chair assistants and collectors. The cost of this would have been much more than the Band was earning and collecting at the time, so the proposal was dropped.

In 1927 Mr Traversi introduced community singing concerts into his winter concert season, on 12th February. It was such a success that it became a feature of the summer promenade season too. Huge numbers of song-sheets were purchased from various publishers, including national newspapers such as the Daily Express, who were promoting the idea of community singing at that time. The song-sheets were given free to members of the audience and contained the lyrics to popular songs of the day. On some evenings, Mr Traversi invited members of the audience to the stage to croon a tune with the Band, the audience then voting for the contestants by a show of hands.

Mr Traversi then introduced hymn-singing evenings, at which hymns were sung in both English and Welsh. But unlike today hymns were not played on Sundays; the church authorities were afraid people would prefer to perform their devotions on the promenade rather than attending local churches. In the early 1930s hymns were sung as part of the Band's afternoon concerts in the Happy Valley.

The community singing, in particular, led to complaints from some of the hotels near the bandstand about the noise and the huge crowds overflowing the promenade. As a result, community singing was kept to two concerts a week.

Mr Traversi may have had an ulterior motive for promoting these concerts: tax avoidance! Entertainment Duty was payable on any admission charges over 3d for listening to a concert. As the

Aug 1942

"Holidays at Home" Community Singing.

Communityland
No. 1.

Music of this Selection,
of all Music
Dealers and of the Copyright
Owners—B. Feldman & Co.,
125-7-9 Shaftesbury Avenue,
London, W.C.2

1. Fall In and Follow Me.

Fall in and follow me!
Fall in and follow me!
Come along and never mind the
weather,
All together, stand on me, boys ;
I know the way to go,
I'll take you for a spree,
You do as I do and you'll be right,
Fall in and follow me.

2. Another little Drink won't do us any harm.

Another little drink, another little
drink,
Another little drink wouldn't do
us any harm.
Another little drink, another little
drink,
Another little drink wouldn't do
us any harm. (Repeat)

3. Down at the Old Bull and Bush.

Come come, come and make
eyes at me,
Down at the old Bull and Bush,
Come, come, drink some port
wine with me
Down at the old Bull and Bush,
Hear the little German Band,
Just let me hold your hand, dear.
Do, do come and have a drink or
two
Down at the old Bull and Bush.

4. I do like to be beside the Seaside.

Oh ! I do like to be beside the
seaside,
I do like to be beside the sea ;
I do like to stroll upon the Prom,
Prom, Prom,
Where the brass bands play
Tiddely-ly-om pom-pom !
So just let me be beside the sea-
side,
I'll be beside myself with glee,
And there's lots of girls beside
I should like to be beside,
Beside the seaside ! Beside the
sea !

5. It's a long, long way to Tipperary !

It's a long way to Tipperary,
It's a long way to go ;
It's a long way to Tipperary
To the sweetest girl I know !
Good-bye, Piccadilly !
Farewell, Leicester Square !
It's a long, long way to Tipperary,
But my heart's right there.

6. Hello ! Hello ! Who's your Lady Friend ?

Hello ! Hello ! who's your lady
friend ?
Who's the little girlie by your
side ?
I've seen you with a girl or two,
Oh ! oh ! oh ! I am surprised at
you !
Hello ! hello ! stop your little
games,
Don't you think your ways you
ought to mend ?

It isn't the girl I saw you with at
Brighton,
Who, who, who's your lady
friend ?

7. Just a Wee Deoch an Doris.

Just a wee deoch-an-doris,
Just a wee yin that's a',
Just a wee deoch an-doris,
Before we gang awa'.
There's a wee wife waitin',
In a wee but-an-ben ;
If you can say, "It's a braw bricht
moonlicht nicht,"
Ye're a' richt, ye ken.

8. I'm Twenty-one To-day.

I'm twenty-one to-day !
Twenty-one to-day !
I've got the key of the door,
Never been twenty-one before,
And Pa says I can do as I like,
So shout Hip, hip, hooray !
He's a jolly good fellow,
Twenty-one to-day. (Repeat.)

9. If You were the only Girl in the World.

If you were the only girl in the
world,
And I were the only boy,
Nothing else would matter in the
world to-day,
We would go on loving in the
same old way,
A Garden of Eden just made for
two,
With nothing to mar our joy :
I would say such wonderful things
to you,
There would be such wonderful
things to do,
If you were the only girl in the
world,
And I were the only boy.

10. Mademoiselle from Armentières.

Mademoiselle from Armentières,
Parley-voo !
Mademoiselle from Armentières,
same to you !
Who was the girl who lost her
sheep
Thro' singing this chorus in her
sleep ?
Mademoiselle from Armentières !

11. By the side of the Zuyder Zee.

By the side of the Zuyder Zee,
Zuyder Zee, Zuyder Zee,
There my Deutcher girl waits for
me, only me !
I've seen diamonds in Amsterdam,
Amsterdam, Amsterdam ;
But there's not a diamond as
bright as those eyes by the
Zuyder Zee.

12. Take me back to dear old Blighty.

Take me back to dear old Blighty,
Put me on the train for London
Town.
Take me over there, drop me
anywhere,
Liverpool, Leeds or Birmingham,
Well, I don't care !
I should love to see my best girl,
Cuddling up again we soon should
be,
Whoa ! Tiddley iddley ighty,
Hurry me back to Blighty,
Blighty is the place for me.

Communityland
No. 2.

Music of this Selection,
of all Music
Dealers and of the Copyright
Owners—B. Feldman & Co.,
125 7 9 Shaftesbury Avenue,
London, W.C.2.

1. Put Me amongst the Girls.

Put me amongst the girls !
Put me amongst the girls !
Do me a favour, do,
You know I'd do as much for you,
Put me amongst the girls,
Those with the curly curls ;
They'll enjoy themselves and so
will I
If you put me amongst the girls !

2. Oh ! You Beautiful Doll.

Oh ! you beautiful doll,
You great big beautiful doll !
Let me put my arms about you,
I could never live without you ;
Oh ! you beautiful doll,
You great big beautiful doll !
If you ever leave me,
How my heart will ache,
I want to hug you,
But I fear you'd break.
Oh, oh, oh, oh,
Oh ! you beautiful doll !

3. She's a Lassie from Lancashire.

She's a lassie from Lancashire,
Just a lassie from Lancashire,
She's a lassie that I love dear,
Oh ! so dear !
Tho' she dresses in clogs and
shawl,
She's the prettiest of them all,
None could be fairer or rarer than
Sarah,
My lass from Lancashire !

4. Oh ! It's a lovely War.

Oh ! oh ! oh ! it's a lovely war,
Who would n't be a soldier, eh ?
Oh ! it's a shame to take the pay,
As soon as "reveille" has gone
We feel just as heavy as lead,
But we never get up till the ser-
geant brings
Our breakfast up to bed.
Oh ! oh ! oh ! it's a lovely war,
What do we want with eggs and
ham,
When we've got plum and apple
jam ?
Form fours ! right turn !
How shall we spend the money
we earn ?
Oh ! oh ! oh ! it's a lovely war.

5. Nellie Dean.

There's an old mill by the stream,
Nellie Dean,
Where we used to sit and dream,
Nellie Dean,
And the waters as they flow
Seem to murmur sweet and low,
You're my heart's desire,
I love you, Nellie Dean.

6. Sing us a Song of Bonnie Scotland.

Sing us a song of Bonnie Scotland,
Any old song will do.
Round the old camp fire,
A rough and ready choir
Will join in chorus too.
You take the high road
And I'll take the low ;
Let's sing that we all know.

'Twill remind the boys of Bonnie
Scotland,
Where the heather and the blue-
bells grow.

7. I want to be in Dixie.

I want to be, I want to be,
I want to be down home in Dixie,
Where the hens are a-dog-gone
glad to lay
Scrambled eggs in the new mown
hay.
You ought to see, you ought to see,
You ought to see my home in
Dixie.
You can tell the world I'm goin'
to D-I-X,
I don't know how to spell it,
But I'm goin' you bet I am goin'
To my home in Dixieland.

8. A Bird in a Gilded Cage.

She's only a bird in a gilded cage,
A beautiful sight to see,
You may think she's happy and
free from care,
She's not, tho' she seems to be,
'Tis sad when you think of her
wasted life,
For youth cannot mate with age,
And her beauty was sold for an
old man's gold,
She's a bird in a gilded cage.

9. I was Standing at the Corner of the Street.

And for standing at the corner of
the street,
They dress'd me up, with spurs
upon my feet ;
They put me on a horse's back to
teach me how to ride ;
When I fell off the riding master
came to me and cried :
" How ever did you come to be a
soldier ? " I replied :
" I was standing at the corner of
the street ! "

10. If I should Plant a Tiny Seed of Love.

If I should plant a tiny seed of love
In the garden of your heart,
Would it grow to be a great big
big love some day,
Or would it die and fade away,
Would you care for it and tend it
ev'ry day,
Till the time when all must part,
If I should plant a tiny seed of love
In the garden of your heart.

11. Molly O'Morgan.

Molly O'Morgan with her little
organ,
Was dressed up in colours so gay.
Out in the street ev'ry day,
Playing "Too-ra-li-oo-ra-li-oo-ra-
li-ay !
Poor little Molly who met her could never
forget her,
She set all their hearts in a whirl,
Molly O'Morgan with her little
organ,
The Irish Italian Girl !

12. Ship Ahoy !

All the nice girls love a sailor,
All the nice girls love a tar ;
For there's something about a
sailor,
Well, you know what sailors are.
Bright and breezy, free and easy,
He's the ladies' pride and joy ;
Falls in love with Kate or Jane,
Then he's off to sea again,
Ship ahoy ! ship ahoy !

'Community singing' was an activity much promoted in the national press in the 1920s and 30s. Mr Traversi bought thousands of copies of song sheets for distribution to the eager crowds on the Promenade. The 'Community Singing' concerts were so well attended that hotels along the seafront complained about the noise and congestion.

53

Band charged 6d per deck-chair, this counted as a taxable 'admission charge' and the Band would have to pay the duty. However, the duty was 'zero rated' if the audience paid to take part in the concert – a fine distinction. The sums involved were quite large - in 1932, even including a large number of 'zero-rated' concerts, the duty payable for the season totalled £53.15s.3d. Whether audience participation was actually introduced as a means of avoiding the tax is unknown, but the community singing concerts turned out to be some of the most popular of all.

Receipts rose year by year and the bandmaster was regularly congratulated by the Band Committee on each season's successes. His salary gradually rose – in 1926 he received £100, plus £22 bonus, although subsequent seasons only yielded £10 bonus.

The Wider World

There are occasional references in the minutes to other political events affecting the Band: the early days of the 1921 season (June) saw only small audiences, due to the Coal Strike (89 days, ending 28th June). Similarly, the early part of the 1926 season was a little lean due to 'the country's industrial trouble' – the General Strike, 4th-12th May, followed by the continuing Miners' Strike. The strike was blamed for a delay in the return of a Band uniform tunic, which had been sent to the Uniform Clothing and Equipment Company in London for alteration.

On 7th July 1929 the Band gave a concert in thanksgiving for the recovery of King George V. The King had been taken seriously ill the previous year with blood poisoning of the lung, and had deteriorated to the point where David the Prince of Wales was recalled from a visit to South Africa, just in case. However, an operation to drain the lung was successful and the King slowly recovered. The Band's programme included the overture 'Light Cavalry', selections of melodies by Gilbert and Sullivan and Tchaikovsky, a trombone solo played by Harry Edwards and a euphonium solo featuring Robin H. Williams.

In December the same year the Great Depression was evidently beginning to bite, as the Band and other artistes gave their services free of charge for a concert at the Palladium Theatre. The concert raised £22.17s.6d in aid of the Unemployment Appeal Fund. Two years later the economic situation was still poor, and with visitor numbers reduced the 1932 summer concerts were suspended for a two week period after Whit because of low receipts.

There were doubtless many local events in which the Band was involved, but we only have records of a few of them. In 1926 a band contest was organised as part of the Conway Bridge Centenary Celebrations 1826-1926. Mr Traversi advised on the arrangements, and there will also have been parades and ceremonial to mark the occasion. In 1927 Llandudno Band received an appeal from their neighbour, the Penrhynside Band, which was in debt and struggling to keep its players; Llandudno Band took the lead in a benefit concert on 11th December. In 1929 Mr Traversi organized a band contest at The Palladium theatre on 22nd June, and in the evening conducted a concert by the massed bands of Llandudno, Royal Oakeley and Shotton Bands.

The Performing Rights Saga

Mr Traversi's anger was aroused by several subjects through the years and caused him to engage in protracted correspondence with various antagonists. One such was the new Performing Right Society, founded in 1914 to secure royalties for composers for performances of their works. Any establishment that put on entertainment had to purchase a performing licence, to pay royalties to composers and publishers who had opted in to the scheme. Mr Traversi did not agree with this, either because he genuinely felt that bands should be able to play works in public freely, or because he did not want add to the costs of running the Band.

In the early days not all publishers joined the scheme, and it was quite easy to buy only pieces of music that could be performed without restriction. Many publishers were themselves opposed to any restrictions on performance of their works, and even some of the largest entertainment houses did not wish to be liable for any extra fees – in 1923 the Winter Gardens at Blackpool warned artistes not to perform anything controlled by any Performing Right Society. The campaign was led for a while by B. Feldman and Co., Music Publishers, and was even known as 'Feldmanism'.

But, gradually, as the early twenties passed, all of the brass band publishers signed up to the PRS, and Mr Traversi could not obtain the latest popular tunes for his Band from unaffiliated publishers. The choice was: pay an annual charge and freely perform anything controlled by the PRS, or keep records of everything played during the year and only pay a fee for each controlled item – an onerous task. Thus, in May 1926 Mr Traversi requested the Council to obtain a general licence covering the Town Hall and the promenade, to enable the Band to play any music they liked.

Some years later, a diligent policeman noticed that the Band was not displaying its Performing Rights licence disc on the bandstand during the evening performance; the Council therefore had to prosecute the management of the Band (i.e. the Council itself) for the breach of licence, and was fined £5!

Unfair Competition

Mr Traversi was a great champion of local bands and musicians, and strove continually to improve the quality and competence of bands in North Wales. He was a founder member of the North Wales Brass Band Association (NWBBA) and was an outspoken critic of anything that, he felt, impaired the progress of the band movement.

He was convinced that local players were suffering a disadvantage due to an exemption in the rules governing band contests; no doubt originally designed to assist bands who had an insufficient number of their own players, the rule allowed bands to borrow players from other bands for contests. He wrote eloquent letters to the 'Welsh Notes' page of the 'British Bandsman' newspaper to initiate and pursue a campaign to get the rule changed. In August 1923 he wrote:

'The National Eisteddfod, for instance, insert a rule stating that each band will be allowed four outsiders, with a result that most bands, fearing the others are going to do the same, import soloists from England for the contest, and the Welsh boys are made to stand down. The effect of all this is that North Wales has no soloists of any note, and they never will produce first-class players...

'...Look at what happened at Cemaes Bay [contest]. [*Holyhead Band had borrowed from top bands Foden's, Kingston Mills and others*]. What about the efficiency of Holyhead Band the day after the contest? In all probability the contest did more harm to the band than good. Llandudno Band, on the other hand – no imports from England – were the same band the day after the event, and all the soloists benefited by the experience of the test.

'...Notwithstanding the universally accepted fact that Wales is a musical nation, we cannot 'hold a candle' to the English brass instrumentalist. And that is what the National Eisteddfod, more than any other influence, has done to the Band movement of Wales.'

Mr Traversi's letters, and the support of the 'British Bandsman''s columnist, 'Garthowen', resulted in the rules being changed. However, bands still found ways to sneak crack soloists in for the day until eventually a comprehensive band registration system was introduced. This still operates today and prevents a band fielding players who are registered with another band.

The Right Kind of Music

Mr Traversi's third great crusade also concerned band contests: he objected to the kind of music that was being chosen as test-pieces for the various classes of bands. In this dispute the 'British Bandsman''s columnist 'Garthowen' was his opponent rather than his supporter.

'Garthowen' was the pseudonym of Mr W. J. Parry Jones from Menai Bridge, a brass band contest adjudicator and member of the committee of the North Wales Brass Band Association. In 1927 it appears the NWBBA had chosen various test-pieces for contests, selected from a certain music publisher's catalogue.

Mr Traversi felt that the band movement was best served by as many bands as possible taking part in contests. He contended that bands are more likely to enter a contest if they like, and can play, the prescribed test-piece. But the pieces on offer in this particular publisher's catalogue were, in his opinion, too difficult for the local bands. This was discouraging them from taking part, which would soon have a detrimental effect on the whole brass band movement in North Wales.

The dispute continued for over a year and became more and more personal. Mr Traversi intimated more than once that Mr Jones's influence on this subject with the NWBBA, and in the pages of the 'British Bandsman', was inappropriate, even self-interested, as he had an interest in the publishing house in question. 'Garthowen' responded by accusing Mr Traversi of being against 'progressive' music, and calling the more popular style of test-piece 'stinky' music!

There was no winner in the argument, each held to their views, and the choice of contest test-pieces has ever been a source of friction. For many years the top competitions for the Championship section bands have had a new piece of music specially written for the occasion, ever more complicated and technically challenging to test the players' skills and musicianship. Many people do not like these, not considering them to be 'music'. In recent times the North Wales Brass Band Association has not prescribed any particular test-piece for its November Rally, leaving it to the bands' 'own choice' – perhaps Mr Traversi gained his point, after all?

Chapter 5

More Popular than Ever – the 1930s

The town of Llandudno and the Band weathered the Depression of the early 1930s and prospered again as visitor numbers increased. After the relative shortage of funds of the previous few years, the Band Committee found it necessary in 1934 to draw the Council's attention to the state of the Band's uniforms. The current style of uniform had been bought, as a set, in 1918, and it had been the policy to replace individual items as they wore out. The average life of uniform items, under such intensive use, was four or five years; for the 1934 season there were so many replacements needed, the Committee asked for assistance in purchasing a complete new set. They recommended a new style, scarlet tunics with a body belt, dark trousers and a decorated cap. The Council granted £50 towards the total cost of £111. When the bandmaster's uniform was updated in 1938, it cost £5.11s.10d for a frock coat with embroidered collar and a scarlet art silk waist sash.

On the Promenade

Promenade concerts continued to be a prime attraction of the resort. An article in the 'Daily Despatch' of 4th August 1937 includes this paragraph:

'My new Yorkshire friend...told me his favourite evening concert was the brass band on the promenade.

'There's a crooner, one o' t' band. 'E puts 'is euphonium down and starts to croon. Good old-time songs, 'Zuider Zee' an' all that. Ee it's champion. 'E loosens 'is collar an' th' audience 'elps 'im out. By gum, 'e brought t' promenade down!'

The crooner is a gas-meter collector, a versatile member of the Llandudno Brass Band'

The crooner in question was doubtless Robin H. Williams, who, we know from the Band minutes, was seeking a job with the Gas Department in April 1934, and who appears as euphonium-player in the Band list of 1937. The Council often provided day-time employment for musicians - the Gas, Electricity and Surveyor's Departments were favourites - so that they did not leave the town and would be available for Band duty.

The popularity of the promenade concerts, however, often gave rise to complaints. In both 1933 and 1935, the Council wrote to the bandmaster complaining of 'serious congestion .... on the promenade during the band concerts, ... a clear passage of at least 16 feet must be provided between the deck chairs and the promenade continuous seating.'. In 1934 the Imperial Hotel objected to Band collectors coming on to the hotel balcony, 'trespassing on private ground' and 'pestering' their patrons – Mr Traversi replied that collections were only sought there when patrons had requested pieces to be played!

The crooning gas-meter inspector – principal euphonium Robin H. Williams in the 1930s.
(Photo: Baxter's Photography)

The bandstand lighting continued to give problems. When the evenings begin to draw in, from mid-August, the musicians cannot see the music towards the end of the concert, so some sort of lighting is necessary. Concerns were expressed before the permanent bandstand was even completed in 1926, and the inadequacy of the lighting is mentioned in almost every one of Mr Traversi's end-of-season reports. Mr

Harold Morton, the Engineer of the Electricity Works department, was approached yet again in 1936 for floodlighting around the bandstand, but replied that 'In view of all the additional lights in the way of decorations, there would be grave danger of breaking down the promenade lighting cables to make further additions. I therefore cannot undertake it under present conditions.' But at last, according to the bandmaster's report of October 1938, the bandstand lighting had been improved!

On the Wireless
In December 1936 the Band was auditioned by the British Broadcasting Corporation, with a view to a concert being broadcast live on radio. The BBC's representative was satisfied with the performance, and the Band was engaged to perform three seven-minute sessions on 9th February 1937, broadcast live from the Town Hall. A second engagement then followed: on 21st August 1937 a concert at the Pier Pavilion was broadcast from 6.00pm to 6.40pm, the programme consisting of a selection from Rossini's 'Barber of Seville', the 'March of the Manikins' by Fletcher, Rimmer's 'A Patriotic Review', 'The Blue Danube' and 'The Teddy Bears' Picnic'. The fee for this was £15.15s.0d.

The Band played for other BBC broadcasts over a number of years, but unfortunately the BBC are now unable to locate any of these performances – either they were not recorded, or the recordings have been lost.

Almost a Full-Time Job
In today's climate, where hobbies typically absorb one or two evenings a week, or maybe a day or two if you're a golfer or angler, it is difficult to imagine the commitment of these volunteer bandsmen (and their families!). During the season they met every evening, Monday to Saturday – usually over 100 evenings, although the concerts did not always go ahead if the weather was inclement. On these occasions, no fee was paid. Every Sunday there was a concert in the Happy Valley. There were occasionally

weekday engagements, for which some members had to be paid for loss of wages, and numerous other events which would often take up a good part of a Saturday or Sunday:

* May Day carnivals in Llandudno and Colwyn Bay, Rose Day engagements in June, Armistice Day parades;
* Rhos School Sports Days and cricket matches, Woodlands Sports Days, LMS Railway Reception and Sports Days, various garden parties, trade and teachers' conferences;
* Opening of the new tennis courts 1932, opening of the new paddling-pool 1937, laying of foundation stone at the new hospital 1938;
* Royal Welch Fusiliers' reunion 1934, Llewelyn Roberts presentation 1936, the Coronation of King George VI 1937, naming ceremony for a new LMS locomotive 1938;
* Lord Roberts Memorial Fund and other benefit concerts, as well as many 'special' concerts on the promenade, the pier and in the Happy Valley.

The men were still being paid the original rate of 1s.6d per performance, but by the 1930s the end-of-season bonus was being paid at a rate of an extra 2s.6d per attendance. By the end of the decade they were earning an extra £15 each – the Inland Revenue tax return for 1938/39 shows most of them declaring £30 in 'Band wages'.

Personnel Matters
Some of the Band's best-known characters are in evidence in the attendance registers of the 1920s and 1930s. Isaac Williams, who masterminded the metamorphosis of the St Tudno Band into the Llandudno Town Band in 1910, played continuously for 31 seasons until his eventual retirement in 1942. Robin H. Williams, a learner during the First World War, was still playing during the 1930s, and became a member of the Band Committee. He was to become bandmaster in the 1950s. War veterans Reg Williams, Ivor Evans,

With muffled drums, the Band leads the civic procession to the Memorial Service at Holy Trinity Church, Llandudno, on the day of the interment of His Majesty King George V, 28th January 1936.

Peter Price and E.R. Roberts were still going strong at the end of the 1930s, and another, Robert J. Davies, retired in 1937.

Mr Thomas George Brookes joined as a collector in August 1923 and was in the senior Band in 1924 – through him his two sons George and Arthur, and at least six of his nephews joined the Band over the years. The bandmaster's son, Antonio 'Tony' Traversi joined the cornets in 1927, and played solo cornet up until the end of 1940, after which he left to pursue his musical career in other directions (see panel).

The Band Committee minutes of 7th July 1937 record a notable success for one of the Band members: Mr Geoffrey Lindon, who first appears in the attendance register at the beginning of the 1935 season as a learner, was awarded a scholarship to the Trinity College of Music in London to study the trombone. He later enjoyed a long and illustrious career as a symphonic bass trombonist with the London Symphony Orchestra, the BBC Symphony Orchestra and the BBC Concert Orchestra.

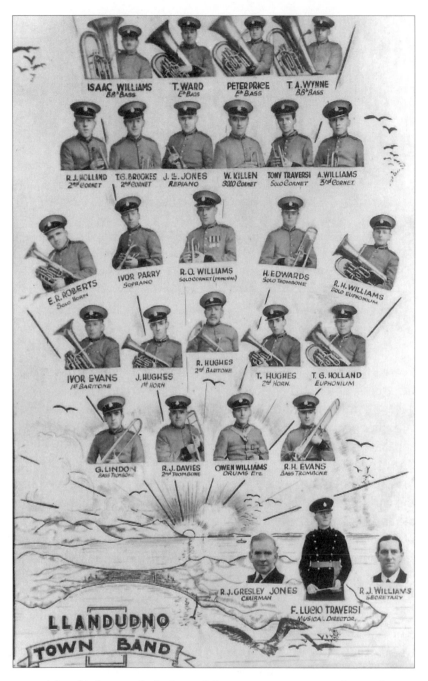

A band to be proud of – in 1936 the summer programme featured photographs of the players. (Photo: Baxter's Photography)

The stage at Happy Valley is more commonly associated with minstrel shows, the Concord Follies and Alex Munro, but it should not be forgotten that the Llandudno Town Band played here most Sunday afternoons from 1911 until well into the 1970s. (Photo: Conwy Archive Service)

Mr Traversi was proud of the Llandudno Town Band's 'home-grown' talent, all of the players being local men 'trained in our own bandroom'. He did not agree with the practice of borrowing players from other bands for important engagements. He felt so strongly about this that he even turned down an ex-Black Dyke Mills Band solo cornet player who wrote for a job in the Band, replying that he did not want a player who would stay with the Band for only a season or two before moving on elsewhere!

Antonio 'Tony' Battista Traversi

Mr Traversi's eldest son, Antonio ('Tony'), was born in 1915 and began playing the cornet and piano at a very early age. He joined his father in the Llandudno Town Band when he was only ten. He was extraordinarily musically gifted, having perfect pitch (the instinctive ability to recognise and produce the correct note without reference to any external standard), the mastery of any style of music on the piano and a talent for composition. Many were the arguments in the Traversi household when his father disapproved of the style or structure of the composition in progress. Tony Traversi was the composer of the march 'The Great Orme', which is featured on the Llandudno Town Band's compact disc of the same name.

During the 1940s and 50s Tony ran the very popular Tony Traversi Orchestra in Llandudno. He was considered a little eccentric, but his quirkiness paid dividends when in 1961 he was invited to join

Sid Millward and The Nitwits - Tony Traversi extreme left

Sid Millward's band, the Nitwits, as pianist for their contract at The Stardust Hotel, Las Vegas. The Nitwits were 'ten wonderful, nonsensical, motley musical entertainers' who brought the Stardust's show to a hilarious conclusion each night. Tony fitted in perfectly with his talent for playing any instrument you can think of (and quite a few made-up ones, too) and his zany sense of humour.

The show alternated between Las Vegas and the Paris Lido for ten years, and then Tony formed his own comedy orchestra, 'Nuts and

Bolts', with Bob Flag and Ronald Regan. As Professor Nuts, Tony performed for over thirty years in various incarnations of the group, with Cyril Lagey, Howie Morgan, Dave Pogson, Stan Van Hoorn, Tommy Shand and Joe Chisolm. Their particular brand of musical slapstick featured scores of different instruments, many of them invented by Tony, such as his classic serpent trumpet and the toilet-trombone. He could also repair anything, usually with a wire coathanger and a piece of string!

'Nuts and Bolts' were great favourites all over the UK, Europe and beyond. They performed alongside stars such as Bob Hope, Bing Crosby, The Smothers Brothers, Little and Large and Les Dawson.

Nuts and Bolts with instruments

They played the single season of Barnum and Bailey's Kaleidoscape in the United States and then went on to star with Circus Roncalli in Germany.

Tony Traversi's last performance was at The Opera House, Blackpool, with Ken Dodd in 2003. 'The Grand Old Man of British Comedy' died in Chingford on March 26 2004, aged 89.

For further information, visit www.nutsandboltscomedy.com

(Photos: Nuts and Bolts Comedy)

Professor Nuts

Chapter 6

The Second World War, 1939-1945

The autumn of 1939 was a particularly turbulent time for the Llandudno Town Band. Firstly, and most obviously, war broke out on 3rd September and brought the season to an abrupt halt, just as the Band was making up the financial loss caused by poor weather earlier in the summer. Secondly, it lost its secretary, and thirdly, it lost its bandmaster.

Mr R. J. Williams had been the Band secretary and treasurer for at least 15 years, but it appears that during 1939 certain irregularities in his accounting, amounting to £60, had come to light. He was also connected with the Llandudno Urban District Council, Maesdu Golf Club and North Wales Golf Club, where more discrepancies were discovered, and it was decided by all of these organisations to institute criminal proceedings. Mr Williams resigned from his office with the Band in October 1939, and from then on the Band accounts were independently audited each year. Mr E. Norman Jones took over as secretary the following year.

The loss of the bandmaster, by contrast, was only technical and temporary, and not caused by a fall from grace. Due to the Council's superannuation scheme, Mr F. Lucio Traversi's contract as electricity meter inspector and town bandmaster came to an end on 30th September 1939, in his 66th year. This would necessitate the Band Committee appointing a new bandmaster. The Band evidently did not want to replace Mr Traversi, so the Council decided to assist the Band by contributing an extra £100 a year so that the Band Committee itself could employ a bandmaster, rather than the Council finding him daytime employment. This enabled the Committee to reappoint the now-retired Mr Traversi.

The Show Goes On

With the outbreak of hostilities many people and essential services were evacuated from London and other vulnerable areas. Llandudno was the recipient of several Government departments, relocated well away from enemy bombing. The resulting influx of 'visitors' brought an unexpected boost to the town's fortunes at a time when most folk were not contemplating summer holidays. Accordingly, the Band Committee decided that it would be 'business as usual' for the Band in 1940, and concerts began on Saturday 11th May.

The wartime lighting restrictions meant that the summer concerts began progressively earlier in the evenings after 5th August, but Mr Traversi was able to report on 7th October that, although earlier concerts coincided with hotels' dinner-times, large numbers of people had still managed to attend and receipts were stable. But, as he pointed out to the Band Committee, 'I would like to add a word on the matter of the result of our efforts:- The chief function of the Band is to add to the amenities and attractions of the town, therefore the financial aspect should be regarded as of secondary importance. Even if we should end with heavy loss, this would be compensated for in the knowledge that the many thousands of visitors who stroll along the promenade during the summer months derive no small measure of enjoyment and inspiration from the music discoursed by the Llandudno Town Band.'

Mr Traversi also recorded his 'deep appreciation to the members of the Band, who in most trying circumstances exerted their special efforts to carry on with the job of providing the visitors with wholesome and cheerful entertainment at a time when it is of such paramount need. On occasions members actually came straight from their work of national importance to the bandstand and deferred their evening meal until after the performance. The majority put in 100% of attendance and those who missed a concert or two occasionally were prevented from appearing on account of the importance of the work on which they are engaged.'

Requisitioned for the Cause

But it was not long before the Band had to make sacrifices; as a consequence of the Government's plans for the extension of fire prevention services, the Band's practice room above the fire station, which had been in use for thirty years, was commandeered as a dormitory for duty officers of the Central Fire Station. Another

room was found for the Band, a former storeroom above the electricity sub-station in Georges Street, but it was far from ideal. It was small, cold and dark, and the floor was made of a rather soft concrete which gave off coarse and damaging dust. There were pleas for better lighting and heating and for permission to expand into the room next door for storage of instruments, as Mr Traversi was sure that

The Second World War, and a depleted Llandudno Town Band leads a detachment of the Fire Service along Mostyn Street, photographed from the top of a Llandudno tram. The war caused a huge mobilisation of personnel, and there were many opportunities for people to serve their country, both nationally and locally. For example, the Grand Inaugural Procession of 'Wings for Victory' Week included detachments from the National Fire Service, the A.R.P. Warden service, the A.R.P. Decontamination Service, the A.R.P. Rescue and Demolition service, the Civil Defence Casualty service, the British Red Cross and St John detachments, Women's Land Army, Women's Voluntary Service, Coast Watchers, Lifeboat crew, Boy Scouts, Girl Guides, as well as R.A.F. and A.T.C. personnel, Home Guard and Royal Regiment of Artillery.

the 'uninviting,' 'cramped' and 'soulless' conditions were discouraging some players from attending winter rehearsals. But in the absence of anything better, this room was used as a headquarters until 1948.

In late 1940 the Band was threatened with a very serious blow – the promenade bandstand was earmarked as a sea-front machine-gun post. Plans had been under discussion between the Council and the military authorities since at least August 1940 to construct a number of gun emplacements along the coast, from the Little Orme to the District boundary at Deganwy. Some of these concrete structures were to be hidden in the landward side of the small shelters along the promenade, another was to be on the seaward side of the paddling-pool near Bodafon Fields. Item 5 on the list of proposed locations reads:

'On the deck of the Bandstand, Gloddaeth Crescent.
(This will practically render its use for Band purposes void, unless a temporary extension is made on to the promenade).'

In consternation, the Band Committee 'unanimously resolved that representations be made to the Council in committee to make strong representations to the military authorities against the taking over of the Bandstand'. This appeal must have been successful; nothing further is mentioned in the minutes in later months, and the summer season went ahead as normal. Indeed, there seems to be no evidence that any of the proposed gun emplacements were ever built, other than the Royal Artillery's Coastal Gunnery School on the Great Orme, as the threat of an enemy invasion receded.

But the biggest threat, of which Mr Traversi with his previous wartime experience was all too aware, was the matter of personnel – the Band would lose players through enlistments and war-related work. Already by October 1940 four players had enlisted in the Forces – T. George Holland (euphonium), Alex Williams (horn), J. Glyn Davies (cornet) and Thomas A. Wynne (bass), followed by Henry Davies in December. In addition, the solo trombonist Harry Edwards also resigned, and veterans Reg Williams, P\ ɔr Price and Ivor Evans joined the Home Guard. The loss of so ᵤany players inevitably caused havoc, with some remaining bandsmen having to change instruments to cover the key positions, and other chairs left vacant. The lack of a sufficiently competent solo cornet forced Mr Traversi himself to reluctantly resume his old practice of playing the cornet, left-handed, whilst conducting. The trombone section was sometimes assisted by Mr A.J. Palmer, a serviceman stationed at one of the Llandudno batteries. But the only solution, if the Band was to continue as it

In November 1940 Mr Traversi (rear, left) started his first emergency learners' band of the war. After only five weeks he considered the group competent enough to appear in public, playing Christmas carols.
Back row, left to right: F.L. Traversi, Griff Hughes, Glyn Jones, George H. Brookes;
Middle row: Johnny Price, Ronnie Martin, Johnny Boole, Gordon Thomas, Geraint Hunt;
Front row: David Hughes, Arthur Hingley, John Longworth, Basil Breeze, Francis Jones.
(Photo: Llanrhos Studio and Post Office)

had done during the First World War, was to train more youngsters.

The Junior Band

Mr Traversi began his first learners' class in early November 1940. The twelve boys met to practice on two evenings a week. They were either exceptionally gifted or they had an inspired tutor, for after only five weeks Mr Traversi considered they had made such satisfactory progress that he would allow them to appear in public, as a unit, during the Christmas season. The group played its first concert on Boxing Day 1940, and on 31st May 1941 turned out in its own right for Colwyn Bay May Day Festival.

Mr George H. Brookes was one of the class of 1940. He recalls that Mr Traversi was very strict: he had an ebony ruler, and anyone who played a wrong note would feel it rapping across his knuckles – progress through pain, indeed! After only six months, seven of the boys, including George, moved up to the senior combination (the main Band); eight senior players had now been lost to war service, but with the help of the juniors the Band was at full strength for the 1941 summer season. The boys were only paid at half-rate to start with (2s.6d per appearance, instead of 5s), but even this was a nice bit of pocket money and an attractive incentive for other budding instrumentalists.

A second learners' class was started in the autumn of 1941. By the summer of 1942 there were only ten or eleven senior players available for most engagements, the deficit being made up by juniors. Mr Traversi described the juniors as being the 'backbone' of the combination. In time, though, even the promoted juniors themselves began to enlist in the Forces – further learners' classes were started in 1942, 1943 and 1944.

Several of the learners who joined during the war went on to play in the Band for many years, including Arthur Hingley, James Grundy, Elfyn Roberts, W. J. 'Billy' Jones, Ken Roberts, Thomas Jones, David A. Jones, and Roy Williams. Five brothers of the Hughes family, Griffith, David, James, Hugh and John, joined alongside their cousin George Brookes and his brother Arthur. One of the senior players who decided to finally hang up his uniform in 1942 was Isaac Williams, who had been a member of the St Tudno Band from 1907, and had steered the Band through the 1910 takeover. Another veteran, Richard Hughes, had been in the Band for 54 years and was still a member of the Band Committee.

Patriotic Duties

Mr Traversi considered the Band to be a provider of 'enjoyment and inspiration', and the second of these functions was frequently fulfilled in the many parades and morale-boosting events of the war years. Any civic occasion had a parade, involving members of the military, Home Guard and other uniformed services. There were many fundraising initiatives to buy equipment for the armed

"Warship Week" 1941, and the Band leads a parade past the Town Hall on Lloyd Street. Already there are several young boys in the Band, taking the places of senior members involved in war service. The Week's fundraising efforts resulted in the commissioning of a 656-ton Bangor-class minesweeper, named HMS Llandudno.

forces, and the Band was always in the forefront of local campaigns. November 1940 saw 'War Weapons Week', which included a procession and service at the Pier Pavilion. The 'Warship Week' effort of November 1941 eventually resulted in the commissioning of *HMS Llandudno*, a 656-ton Bangor-class minesweeper, built that year. She served most of the war near Iceland and off the south coast of England, before being sold by the Navy in 1947. The 'Wings for Victory' week, May 1943, sought to raise £180,000 to buy 3 Lancaster bombers and 12 Typhoon fighter planes. Another event was 'Salute the Soldier' in July 1944, and in 1945 the Band contributed to efforts for the Youth Improvement Fund and the Welcome Home Fund.

For the first time in history, due to the new wireless technology of radio, people on the Home Front could send their messages and support directly to troops overseas via 'British Empire Broadcasts'. On 5th July 1943 the BBC broadcast a concert from the Grand Theatre, Llandudno, entitled 'Llandudno Calling', which featured the Llandudno Town Band under F. Lucio Traversi, and Llandudno Choral Society under Ffowc Williams. The half-hour programme included 'Men of Harlech' and other marches from the Band, and two items from the choir. Councillor W. H. Pearson, JP, Chairman of the Council, gave an address of support, sending greetings from the town to all service personnel but particularly to those from Wales and from Llandudno itself. The programme ended with choir and audience singing the hymn,'Come, Thou Fount of Every Blessing', to the tune 'Hyfrydol'.

During the 1943 season more players departed for various services: John Hughes, who had been in the band for 25 years, J. Llewelyn Jones (26 years service), Robert 'Bobby' J. Holland (17 years service), Robert Williams (junior member, 6 months), Griffith Hughes (junior member, 3 years). Such was the shortage of players that Mr Isaac Williams came out of retirement in the July and helped out until the end of the season.

Juniors in Hot Water!

All this time the juniors had been doing sterling work, some of them now playing in the senior band, others selling programmes, collecting money and helping with the deck-chairs and equipment. In 1944 this got the Band into trouble on two counts. Firstly, the Llandudno Free Church Council objected that the boys were absent from Sunday School and evening services, thus being 'deprived of spiritual guidance'. Secondly, one of the young musicians had evidently bragged to his friends that he earned good money for playing in the Band, and this reached the ears of the School Attendance Officer.

Some of the juniors on the Council Field (behind 'The Tins') in 1944-45:
Back row, left to right: George Brookes, Glyn Jones, David Hughes,
Elfyn Roberts;
Front row, Jim Hughes, David Lloyd Jones, Hugh Hughes, Ken Roberts,
David A. Jones.

In spite of the support of two Headmasters, Mr Ffowc Williams and Mr R. Lloyd Jones, and a petition from the parents as to the educational, moral and cultural value of the boys' musical

76

activities, it was decided that the byelaws regarding employment of children and young persons were being breached. Although the Director of Education sympathized with the Band's position, the law had to be observed and boys below the age of fourteen could no longer play with the Band.

This left the Band short of players, but eventually, two boys, David J. Lloyd Jones and James Hughes, were actually issued with special licenses to enable them to continue to play; presumably the Band was quite crippled without their particular instruments. To avoid this problem in future, Mr Traversi tried teaching a class of older learners, who would be fourteen by the time they would be ready to join the senior Band. But

Due to the loss of several players through war service, Mr Traversi again took up his cornet to supplement the juniors of the cornet section. He would play left-handed while conducting with his right.

he later reported that they lost interest; in his opinion it was no good starting a boy after the age of twelve!

Mr Traversi's Extra Efforts

Now that he was no longer working during the day, Mr Traversi could spend all his time caring for his beloved Band. In May 1942 he was awarded an extra £25 bonus by the Band Committee in recognition of all the extraordinary activities and services he had taken on. Not only was he training the juniors himself, he was also providing up to a dozen of them with instruments that he owned himself, not all of which were returned to him in the same condition he lent them out. On the bandstand, the practice had been for Robin H. Williams to compere the concert, for which he was paid extra; due to Robin being engaged in war work, Mr Traversi was now compering, but without any extra allowance.

The Band's special concerts were often advertised by means of large posters, hand-made by Mr Traversi himself, using any materials he could lay his hands on. His son, also Francis L. Traversi, remembers his father attending band competitions even before the war, where he would visit the printers who made the huge hoarding posters advertising the contest. He invariably returned home with a large roll of surplus posters under his arm. He would then cut out the pictures of band players from the posters to use on his own creations. In later years, as his eyesight failed and he became more frail, Mr Traversi would ask his son to help him with the lettering of the posters. The younger F. L. Traversi eventually had a poster-making business of his own in Llandudno for many years.

Mr Traversi spent countless hours organizing the players' sheets of music into books. Eventually, each player had 36 books – 936 books in total – all assembled and bound by hand by the bandmaster. Several of these volumes are still in the bandroom. Many years of constant use have left the music books battered and worn.

When Mr Traversi began his career as bandmaster in 1910, the Band had only a very small library of music. He invested in new pieces straight away. Over the years he bound all the sheets of music into books for each individual member of the Band. By the 1940s this library ran to 36 sets of books, i.e. 36 books for the solo cornet, 36 books for the 1st trombone, etc.; 26 players in the band, 936 books in total. This amounts to about 2,234 pieces of music per player, every leaf glued in by hand, and each of the 36 books then bound by hand....and all at his own expense. Many of these sets of books are still in the bandroom, a monument to one man's dedication.

The Band leads a parade of service personnel along the The Parade during "Salute the Soldier" Week in July 1944. Most of the players are juniors, and the trombonist in Army uniform is A.J. Palmer, who was stationed at a gun-battery in the town.

Mr Traversi expected the same level of commitment from his players. Missing a rehearsal or engagement was not tolerated – no excuse was accepted, even illness was not admissible unless a doctor's note could be produced. On one occasion Reg Williams took a day-trip on the steamer to the Isle of Man, a service which

Mr Traversi always marched at the rear right corner of the Band. His pupil George H. Brookes is alongside him during this wartime march, with Glyn Jones in Royal Naval Reserve uniform in the next file.

ran from Llandudno at that time. Unfortunately, the ship was late returning and he missed the promenade concert that evening. Some of today's senior Band members can still remember the dressing-down he received from Mr Traversi. Similarly, when the young Hughie Hughes was courting his future wife some years later, he stubbornly insisted on taking a night off for this purpose each week; the Band regularly fined him half-a-crown (2s 6d) for non-attendance, but he always maintained it was worth it!

The End of the War

By late 1944, after the re-invasion of Europe on D-Day, it was clear that the war was going to end in the Allies' favour, sooner or later. The Council and Band were beginning to plan the victory celebrations as early as October, and the Band Committee was hopefully anticipating the return of its absent players during the coming season. In the event, visitors too flooded back to

The Llandudno cenotaph stands at the north end of the promenade and is topped by the flaming grenade of the Royal Welch Fusiliers, who recruited heavily in the town during the Great War. The memorial was inaugurated in 1922 to commemorate 212 local servicemen who gave their lives in that conflict, among them Sidney Albert Edwards, the Town Band's flugel horn player. This photograph was taken before the Second World War memorials to a further 122 men were added to the obelisk.

Llandudno after the end of the war, and even the weather was kinder than usual; 1945 was a record season, with 124 performances on the promenade, 12 concerts in the Happy Valley and 3 benefit concerts. The usual competitions and community singing concerts proved immensely popular, and long queues formed for deck-chairs every evening. Performances continued until 5th October, and the financial surplus, after deduction of expenses, was actually greater than the entire receipts of 1944! The bandsmen were rewarded with the usual bonus of 5s. per concert, plus an extra 2s.6d. per concert in view of such an extraordinary season. Mr Traversi received total bonuses of £125. Peace had broken out with a vengeance.

Chapter 7

After the War, 1945-1952

After the make-do-and-mend, do-it-yourself conditions of the war years, it was time to take stock and re-equip the Band to meet the 1946 season and beyond. The promenade bandstand needed a good overhaul – the music stands and bandstand chairs were repaired or replaced, a public-address system was purchased and installed, and of course that hard-won bandstand lighting had been an early casualty of the Wartime Lighting Regulations. Once more, the minutes record pleas for better lighting and wind-screens.

The uniforms were at the end of their lives, over 10 years old. Repairs had been made during the War, but the suppliers had never been able to guarantee the quality or colour of the cloth and braid; by now, they were a mixed bag. The juniors did not have uniforms that fitted them at all; some of the old ones were altered for them, worn and patched as they were. Unfortunately, the purchase of a new set of uniforms was prevented by post-war rationing.

Enquiries were made to buy Government stock uniforms, but this came to nothing. Then it was discovered that it was permitted to collect loose Clothing Coupons from members of the public and use them to obtain new uniforms. The Chairman of the Band Committee, Mr J.A. Hibbert, and Councillor L.S. Underwood immediately offered six of their own coupons each. An appeal was published in the press for a total of 588 clothing coupons to re-equip the Band. After four months only 254 had been collected, with which only new trousers and caps could be purchased. Collections towards the tunics continued for some time.

Mr Traversi Retires

At the Band Committee meeting of 12th March 1947, Mr Francis Lucio Traversi tendered his resignation as bandmaster of the Llandudno Town Band. He was now 72 years of age and in poor health – of necessity the young George Brookes had been deputising for him at rehearsals during the last few weeks.

'The resignation of the Bandmaster was accepted with sincere regret and it was decided to place on record the Committee's high appreciation of his loyal and devoted services to the Band, to the Town and to the thousands of visitors to Llandudno.'

He was appointed an honorary member of the Band Committee and was asked to sit on the sub-committee formed to appoint his successor. Advertisements for the post were placed in the usual band journals.

Around 140 applicants answered the advertisement, of whom 64 were still sufficiently interested after reading the job description to return the questionnaire sent to them by the recruitment sub-committee. Of these, five were selected for interview. It proved impossible to get everyone to attend on the same day, but by 17th May all had been interviewed and auditioned, and the choice was reduced to either Mr W. J. Connell of Newark, or Mr William Skelton of Rotherham.

'Mr Traversi and the Band representatives were unanimously of the opinion that Mr William Skelton was the most suitable for the post of Bandmaster and had the greater experience of conducting bands.'

Mr Skelton was offered the job and accepted, stating that he could start the following week, the 24th May 1947, at the opening of the new season.

William 'Bill' Skelton

Llandudno's second bandmaster, Mr William Skelton, was a renowned tenor horn soloist. He played for some time with the Callenders Cable Works Band of Erith, Kent, which was a leading band of the 1920s and 30s. In this 1938 photograph he is sixth from the left on the middle row, immediately behind the bandmaster.

William Skelton was a prominent figure in the brass band world at the time. He was born in Biddulph, Staffordshire, on January 13th 1913 and began to play cornet with Biddulph Moor Band at the age of ten. He later moved on to tenor horn and played with several leading bands. His headed notepaper reads 'The Renowned Horn Soloist, Band Teacher and Adjudicator. Late of Luton, Cresswell [Colliery], Callender's [Cable Works] and St Hilda's [Colliery]. Winner of 300 prizes as a soloist.' Evidently Mr Skelton was a player of some ability and with some knowledge of the brass band scene of the day.

Unfortunately, the Council was only able to find temporary daytime employment for Mr Skelton in the Surveyors Department. When that ceased the Band Committee, on a high after two record seasons, decided to pay him £5 per week in addition to his bandmaster's salary of £2 per week, to tide him over until he could find a permanent post. The 1947 season proved to be an incredible record season; the British people were desperate to indulge in a holiday after the wartime privations, and flocked to seaside resorts. The Band recorded a surplus of £1,735! Mr Skelton was granted a special bonus of £150.

William 'Bill' Skelton was bandmaster of the Llandudno Town Band for six seasons, from 1947 to 1952. (From a photo by J. A. Jones)

So, the Band was not short of money, but this did not help them to get their new uniforms. In the aftermath of the war materials were scarce and rationed, and new uniforms could only be obtained by exchanging clothing coupons for Board of Trade vouchers. At last, by October 1947, the Band had had donations of 844 coupons, which enabled the purchase of tunics, trousers, blazers and caps. Even though the old uniforms were in quite a state, they were snapped up by a Lancashire band for £60.

The good fortune continued with the news that the Fire Service was making arrangements to release the requisitioned room above the fire station, and the Band would soon be able to reoccupy it as a bandroom. Unfortunately, the Band then received a bill from the Council for £22.5s. for the rewiring of the room, a bill which the Committee felt should be at least partly borne by the Fire Service.

The 1948 summer season continued the record-breaking trend, and extra bonuses were awarded as before. Mr Skelton was also awarded a bonus of £150 for all his 'additional work during the season'. Unfortunately, this seems to have incensed Mr Traversi, who had always routinely carried out 'additional work' unpaid, such as organising the advertisements in the programmes, making posters, teaching the learners and generally dealing with all correspondence involving the Band. It may have been this payment that prompted him to submit a claim towards the expenses he had incurred over the years in binding the Band's music into books, as mentioned above. Despite several discussions in Committee, and assurances of appreciation of the 'valuable services rendered by Mr Traversi', the request was repeatedly turned down.

A Flurry of Contesting

If we can judge from the headed notepaper mentioned above, Mr Skelton's musical background was evidently one of brass band contests and solo competitions. It should come as no surprise, therefore, to find that he soon entered the Band in more contests than before, and also formed a contesting quartet party. The quartet consisted of Glyn Davies and George Brookes on cornet,

From 1948 thousands of souvenir postcards of the Town Band were sold each year, helping to raise funds and spread its fame far and wide. The photograph was taken on the stage at the Happy Valley, with bandmaster Mr Skelton (inset).
Back row, left to right: Elfed Roberts, Elfyn Roberts, T. George Brookes, Keith Williams, John Hughes, John Ridler, Tommy Jones, Bobby Holland, Owen Williams, Idris Owen, Tom Ward, Ned Roberts, David A. Jones, Arthur Hingley;
Front row: George H. Brookes, Glyn Jones, Jim Hughes, Hughie Hughes, Ken Roberts, James Grundy, Ivor Parry, Dick Hughes, Ivor Evans, Griff Hughes, Reg Williams. (Photo: J. A. Jones)

Contest success

Mr Skelton's quartet parties achieved significant success during 1949:

Deiniolen Eisteddfod:	Senior quartet – First prize Junior quartet – Third prize W. Skelton – Second prize as soloist
Llanrug competition:	Senior quartet – First prize W. Skelton – First prize as soloist Glyn Davies – Second prize as soloist
Haydock competition:	W. Skelton – Second prize as soloist, out of 48 competitors
Northaston competition:	W. Skelton – First prize as soloist, out of 49 competitors Billy Jones – First prize as junior soloist
Prestwich competition:	W. Skelton – Second prize as soloist, out of 50 competitors.
Llandudno competition:	March contest 'C' – First prize and cup March contest 'B' – Second prize Deportment Class 'B' – First prize and music worth £2.2s. Deportment Class 'C' – First prize and music worth £2.2s Selection contest 'C' – First prize, Association Cup and £5.5s.

William Skelton on horn and Arthur Hingley on euphonium. Sometimes the party also included Billy Jones, an up-and-coming youngster on cornet. During the winter of 1948 they competed at a contest at Nelson, Lancashire, being placed fifth out of twenty competitors, and had the distinction of beating the Fodens' No. 2 quartet and other well-known works' bands. They also travelled to Oxford to compete in the Brass Quartet Championship of Great Britain, but without distinction. However, it would have been a valuable experience for the young lads, although at a price – the expenses claim for train fares and two nights' accommodation and meals came to £25.12s.6d.!

In addition, the quartet was auditioned by the BBC at Bangor and were subsequently engaged to perform for several radio broadcasts for a programme entitled 'Ben Bore'. These successes encouraged the full Band to venture into the 'Daily Herald' National Brass Band Contest the following year. The qualifying competition was held at Bolton, and Llandudno were placed fifth out of twenty-one entrants – not high enough to go forward to the finals in London, but 'a very creditable performance considering that the Band had to play without having time for a wash or a drink of tea, (having) been drawn third in order of playing'.

More popular than ever

The Band was by now one of the premier attractions for visitors to Llandudno, but each year several complaints were received that there were insufficient deck-chairs. Queues formed over an hour before the performances began, and the Band had to request permission to use other stacks of Council chairs from further along the promenade. Well over a thousand chairs were set out, filled, and put away again every evening, prompting a revolt by the four deck-chair attendants, led by Mr W.E. Williams, who had much more to do than previously. They were awarded an increase in their pay, to 1s. per concert, but only 'subject to better service being received during the coming season'!

Some Band members were paid special allowances for extra

The Llandudno Senior Quartet carried off the first prize at the Deiniolen Eisteddfod 1949 and enjoyed other successes during the year. Left to right: Arthur Hingley, William Skelton, George Brookes, Glyn Davies.

duties – Jim Hughes received £1 extra for 'singing', and young Billy Jones was paid 10s. for 'whistling' the solo in 'In A Monastery Garden'. In 1948 Mr Skelton introduced the idea of selling postcards of the Band, and thousands of them were produced each year. That first season a total of 8,788 were sold, making a profit of £83 and helping to publicise the Band and the resort far beyond North Wales. But the uniforms needed replacing again in 1951, and the annual profits, although still reasonable, began to fall after the initial post-war boom. The cost of living was increasing rapidly – in 1951, after the purchase of yet another 500 chairs, the chair attendants' pay was increased to 6s.6d. per evening, and 8s. on Sundays. Fortunately the Council acknowledged the Band's importance and helped out by increasing their grants and fees; by 1952 the annual Band grant stood at £300, and the Band received 50% of the profits from Happy Valley concerts.

Those readers who have ever done any marching in a band (particularly trombonists on the front rank) will know what Mr Skelton is saying in this photograph: 'Keep your paces short, we're getting away from the parade!' A band stepping briskly along in time to the music can soon outstrip a May Day procession of floats and artistes on foot. Photo taken on Mostyn Street, Llandudno, between 1947 and 1952.

F. L. Traversi passes away

April 1952 marked, in a quiet way, the end of an era. On the 4th April the band minutes note that Mr F. Lucio Traversi had passed away, and record the Committee's appreciation of his many years' service to the Band. Later that month the secretary and treasurer of the Band, Mr E. Norman Jones, died suddenly and unexpectedly after 12 years service. The post of secretary and treasurer was taken by Robin H. Williams, and so began a new chapter in the history of Llandudno Town Band.

Chapter 8

Show Time on the Promenade
1952-1978

After the 1952 summer season William Skelton resigned from the bandmastership of the Llandudno Town Band. He never had found permanent employment in Llandudno, and this may have been the spur to his moving on – the Band Committee had been finding it more difficult to pay him his £5 a week for the last year. He took up a post with the Falmouth Town Band and enjoyed contest success with them in the Championship section (the 'Premier League' of the brass band world), performing alongside Black Dyke Mills Band at the Royal Albert Hall in 1955.

Robin H. Williams

The baton at Llandudno was taken up on a temporary basis by one of its long-serving members, Mr Robin H. Williams. Born on the Great Orme in 1903, Mr Williams joined as a learner on the cornet in 1913. He then switched to tenor horn and was one of the young lads who formed the 'backbone of the Band' while senior players served their country during the First World War. He entered local government service in 1916, soon transferring to the clerk's department. He then decided to train as a plumber, and he followed this trade for nearly 20 years. In his youth he was quite an athlete, winning gold medals for the 120 yards hurdles and quarter mile in the North Wales championships of 1923.

In 1934 he returned to the Llandudno Urban District Council, working as a gas meter inspector. During the 1930s, in addition to playing the euphonium and leading the community singing, he took on the role of compere on the bandstand; perhaps Mr Traversi, with his hearing difficulties, felt less able to communicate

Mr Robin H. Williams, conductor of the Llandudno Town Band and compere of the promenade shows from 1952 to 1972. His easy style and ready wit encouraged the impromptu performers and kept the audiences enthralled.

effectively with his audience. During the Second World War Mr Williams disappears from the attendance register – he was serving in the Fire Service at Wrexham and Colwyn Bay. Little did his wife know that he often leapt out of windows into a blanket to help train the fire crews! He was later a retained fireman at Llandudno for 20 years. With the end of wartime service he rejoined the Band, and upon the unexpected death of Mr E. Norman Jones in 1952 he took over as secretary and treasurer.

In 1951 he moved to the Clerk's Department at the Town Hall, where he worked until his retirement in 1975. It was a busy enough life, you would think, with every summer evening spent on the bandstand, but added to this he and his wife ran a guest-house in Llandudno.

The Promenade Entertainment Evolves

When Mr Williams took over as bandmaster, the early post-war boom had subsided somewhat and the Band's annual surpluses had turned into losses by 1951. The Council's annual contribution was increased from £200 to £300, but this did not reverse the trend immediately. A band playing well-known tunes on the promenade was still a popular attraction for the visitors, but Mr Williams realised that traditional entertainments would have to change to attract a new generation of holidaymakers. He had seen the great success of the community singing concerts and the conducting and crooning competitions introduced by Mr Traversi; the next step was to introduce even more audience participation.

Over the next few seasons Mr Williams experimented to find a winning formula. Hymn singing on a Sunday evening remained a great favourite, and Mr Williams received letters thanking him for conducting 'so wonderfully and reverently'. For weeknights he introduced more competitions and talent shows. By the late 1950s the week's programme was established as:

Monday: Heats for adult talent competitions (men)
Tuesday: Heats for adult talent competitions (ladies)
Wednesday: Finals of adult talent competitions
Thursday: Children's talent competition and Family Night
Friday: Gala Night, 'The Greatest Laugh on the Promenade', including 'Glamorous Granny' competition, 'Knobbly Knees', etc.

What a success: crowds flocked to the promenade each evening. The entertainment began early, with large numbers of visitors fascinated by the efficiency of the deck-chair attendants putting out over a thousand chairs in record time! The chairs cost 6d. or 1s. and queuing began at least an hour before the show began; all were filled, and visitors frequently wrote to complain that there were not enough. The programme began with some items from the Band, and then the fun would start...

Anyone who wished to sing or dance could choose any music from the Band's library ... and the Band had to bring all of their music with them every evening, all 36 books per man. Various players (particularly the basses!) would lend their

Contestants in the talent competitions were often challenged to play one of the Band's instruments – usually a bass, of course!
(Photo: Llandudno Advertiser)

Under Robin Williams, every night was Show-Night on the promenade. He introduced talent competitions and more audience participation, and for many of Llandudno's visitors the nightly entertainment was the highlight of their holiday. (Photo: J. A. Jones)

instruments for people to try to play them. Some competitions, such as the beauty competitions, had little or no Band involvement at all. Mr Williams was the compere, the axis around which the whole event revolved. He was a showman; visitors loved his jokes and patter, he put people at ease and allowed them to show what they could do. There was rarely a shortage of volunteers to perform on the stage. The following letter is typical of many received at the Town Hall:

'Dear Mr Williams,
I cannot let another hour pass without writing to tell you (and the members of the Band) how much we appreciate all you did to make our visit to Llandudno so very pleasant and memorable. Hearing your gay badinage (helped by the rest of the Band) was one of the highlights of our holiday.

A week ago tonight my blind sister recited 'Betty's Prayer'. You may remember it, it was about an old woman named Betty Brown and her cow? My sister was nervous at 'going up' but you were so kind to her and gave her courage (we were both so grateful to you), but to our great surprise and joy Gladys won the first prize of £3! You can imagine what a thrill that was for her! And now we are back home again, but the memory of our delightful stay there will remain with us always.

You and your fine talented Band will give joy to many visitors to Llandudno this summer, but no one will be more appreciative than my sister (Gladys Preece) and myself. Thank you and bless you all!

Sincerely and gratefully,

Lillian Gray'

With all of the chairs full and collections correspondingly higher, the Band accounts began to look healthier through the 1950s. The exceptions were 1956 and 1957, but this was nothing to do with poor performances; on the contrary, the losses in those years were due to costs incurred through the Band's success...

Robin Williams presiding over the children's competitions on a Thursday night. There was never a shortage of volunteers to take part - one young lad returned for several years in succession and always recited 'The Lion and Albert'!

The Band's talent shows brought visitors flocking to the promenade, as this photograph, taken on 29th July 1960, shows. A thousand deck-chairs would be sold out well before the beginning of the performance, and hundreds more people stood behind to watch. The evening shows were one of the great attractions of the resort. (Photo: J. A. Jones)

The 'Daily Herald' National Brass Band Championship

In 1956 Mr Williams entered the Band in the 'Daily Herald' National Brass Band Championship, a national competition with regional heats. The North West Area qualifying heat took place at the Victoria Hall in Bolton in April. In preparing the test-piece for the competition Mr Williams engaged a well-known professional conductor, Mr Reg Little, to conduct a rehearsal and offer advice and instruction to the players. This must have been helpful as the Band was placed second in the Fourth Section competition. The top two bands in each section qualified for the National Finals in London in the October – Llandudno Town Band was off to the capital!

Congratulations and expressions of support flooded in from other North Wales bands, from the Council and other organisations, and the excitement grew as the summer season

In 1956 Llandudno Town Band entered the 'Daily Herald' National Brass Band Championship of Great Britain, qualifying for the final in London. Excitement and optimism were high as they left Llandudno Station on their way to the capital. (Photo: A. J. Lennie)

drew to a close. The set test-piece was 'Three Songs Without Words', by Eric Ball; Mr Little again helped with training the Band, taking five rehearsals this time, although Robin Williams would conduct at the contest itself. The Final took place on Saturday 27th October and the Band travelled to London by train the day before. The next morning they were up with the lark for a quick run-through and warm-up, and then off to the Highgrove Baths in Shepherd's Bush in time for the draw to determine the playing-order. But a disappointment was in store: Llandudno Band was drawn Number 1, the first band to play, which is always considered to be a disadvantage. There was nothing for it but to play their best and set the standard for everyone else to follow. Amazingly, the adjudicator* considered that only one band improved on that

---

* The adjudicator was Mr T. J. Powell, composer of the famous 'Castell' series of marches, including 'Castell Coch' and 'Castell Caerffili'.

opening performance, and Band No.1 was awarded the second prize in the National Championship – Llandudno Town Band was the second-best Fourth Section band in Britain in 1956!

The prize-winning band of 1956, placed second in the 'Daily Herald'
National Brass Band Championship behind Esh Colliery Band from Durham.
To the left of bandmaster Williams is Bob Edwards, secretary; to the right of
Mr Williams, Cllr. Bob Roberts, Chairman of the Council.
(Photo: Baxter's Photography)

So the financial loss in 1956 was caused by the expenses of the trip and overnight stay in London, and an extra bonus for the bandsmen. And the Band, now promoted to the Third Section, qualified for the London Finals again in 1957! The test-piece was again by Eric Ball, his 'American Sketches', but the Band could not repeat the success of the previous year and was unplaced in the Fourth Section final. After that it was decided not to enter the National competition again; it was an expensive exercise. Llandudno Town Band has never been primarily a contesting band, although some competition out of season is useful for improving the playing standard. Since the days of Mr Skelton and the extraordinary success of 1956, the Band has largely confined itself to entering the annual North Wales Brass Band Association contest each autumn, and an occasional visit to the National Eisteddfod.

A Busy Chap

In 1958 it was remembered that, although Mr Williams had been in charge for six years, his post was officially only 'temporary'; the intention had always been to engage a professional musical director, but somehow this had never happened. Accordingly, advertisements were posted in the band press and Mr Williams resigned his post. There were many applications for the job, including William Skelton, who at this time was with Pontardulais Band in South Wales, but ultimately the Council realised that the promenade entertainment would not be the same without Robin Williams - he was at last offered the post on a permanent basis.

According to his daughters, Robin was 'always going somewhere'; rushing in from work, helping with the serving of the evening meal in the guest-house, dashing out again to the bandroom to lead the Band on to the promenade for the evening performance, all the time being hailed and waylaid by folk eager to chat to one of Llandudno's most popular figures. He was also a leading light in the Llandudno Musical Players, occasionally taking a singing role himself but preferring to direct their musical productions. On several occasions members of the Town Band were drafted in to assist when small onstage bands were required in the show.

During the late 1950s and early 1960s the solo and quartet tradition was revived, and Band members enjoyed frequent successes at various competitions. George H. Brookes often carried off the first solo prize, performing technically difficult 'Airs and Variations' or soulful 'Slow Melodies' on the cornet or euphonium. David A. Jones won a slow melody competition on trombone at

Due to Mr Williams' connections with The Llandudno Musical Players, members of the Town Band sometimes assisted in productions which required onstage musicians. The shows' programme notes: "Any similarity between the village band [in this production] and certain members of a local musical group is entirely intentional, and we wish to thank the members of the Llandudno Town Band who have so generously contributed their time and ability to this production". Above, "Waltz Without End" 1962 at The Palladium; below, "Magyar Melody" 1951 at The Grand Theatre.
Photo (above): John Lawson Reay   Photo (below): Graphic Photos

one Llandudno Festival, but the highpoint was the Llandudno National Eisteddfod of 1963. On this occasion the Brass Quartet prize was awarded to the Llandudno Town Band quartet, conducted by Robin Williams, for their performance of 'Euryanthe' by Weber. The Band's former conductor, William Skelton, was in the audience at the competition; afterwards, ever the perfectionist, he told the players, 'You played it awful, but you were the best there'!

Financial worries

This was an era of mixed fortunes for the Band; on the one hand, their promenade entertainment attracted huge numbers of visitors and fans, and their playing won them prizes and recognition. But throughout the 1960s the balance-sheets at the end of the summer season showed a loss, and each year the deficit grew despite increasing support from the Council.

This was, of course, mainly due to the players being paid for their services, and thus the Band was living beyond its income. But how could one ask these men to attend seven nights a week, without fail, if they were not offered some recompense? These were not professional musicians, but ordinary working men – joiners, painters, plumbers, electricians, shopkeepers. The Band's commitments effectively stifled most other hobbies that they might have taken up, and even family days out at weekends had to be curtailed in order to get back in time for the evening concert. Illness still had to be justified with a doctor's note. For many bandsmen, the day consisted of: a day at work, rush home, serve the evening meal to their visitors (many of them ran a guest-house as a side-line), help with the washing up, dash to the bandstand for the performance and then come home and serve suppers to the guests. Sometimes they managed to fit in a swim from beneath the bandstand at around ten o'clock, after the concert. They could also not take a summer holiday during the promenade season – Band members invariably had to take their holidays in October, when the British weather was starting to turn nasty! David A. Jones even

Five brothers of the Hughes family were players in the Band at various times. Circled here are, left to right, Hughie Hughes, Jim Hughes, Griff Hughes and David Hughes. In addition to playing the cornet, Jim was a noted boy soprano and sang on occasions with John Morava and the Pier Orchestra.

John Hughes, the youngest brother, also played in the Band for some years before moving to London in 1959 to play football professionally with Arsenal. He was on the brink of selection for the first team when he suffered a broken leg in a reserves' match, which ended his career. However, he qualified as a chartered accountant in 1966 and returned to Llandudno and the Band in the 1970s. In the photograph, John Hughes is on the extreme right of the second row down; also in the picture are such famous names as Welsh international Mel Charles (2nd row, 4th from right), Jimmy Bloomfield (3rd row, 3rd from right) and Tommy Docherty (3rd row, 4th from right).

The winning quartet at the National Eisteddfod of 1963, held at Llandudno: W. 'Bill' J. Jones and George H. Brookes (cornets), John J. Edwards (tenor horn) and Hugh Hughes (euphonium), with Robin Williams.
(Photo: John Lawson Reay)

had to delay his wedding until he was free of his playing commitment, but at least his bandsman's bonus paid for the whole of his honeymoon - £12.10s - in London.

But despite the life-style many men still dedicated years to the Band, and some of those from this post-war era played with the Band well into the twenty-first century. Without a core of players such as these brass bands cannot survive, and Llandudno Town Band owes its continuing success to these men, whose lengthy careers have encompassed and overlapped the contributions of many others over the years.

In the early 1980s John Holmes and John Edwards were asked to help set up a band for the Llandudno Boys' Brigade. They ran the band for over ten years and trained many young musicians. On the right of this photograph, holding a bugle, is John Holmes' son Paul, who later played in the Town Band. One of Paul's proudest moments was playing the Last Post alongside his father at the Cenotaph, where his grandfather J. W. Holmes is commemorated as a casualty of the 2nd World War.

An embarrassing moment for Hughie Hughes, as he banged the bass drum rather too enthusiastically during Llandudno's 'Alice in Wonderland' parade in 1982.

Girls!

You will notice that to this point there has been no mention of girls or ladies in the Band. Brass banding was indeed an exclusively male activity. This was perfectly normal all over Britain in that day and age, and the climate did not begin to change until the 1950s and 1960s. Indeed, some brass bands held out against female members even up to the last years of the twentieth century. But nowadays it is not unusual to see bands comprising roughly equal numbers of men and women, or even having a majority of female players. There is certainly no male monopoly on musical talent!

The first lady in the Llandudno Town Band was Miss Julia Etheridge, a local police sergeant. For several years she, John Edwards, John Holmes and John Ridler provided the ceremonial fanfares at the annual appointment of Crown Court judges in Caernarfon.

The first lady member of the Llandudno Town Band was Miss Julia Etheridge, who originally hailed from Tottington near Bury. She joined the Band in 1966 and at various times played cornet and flugel horn. She was a sergeant in the North Wales Police, and

Photograph opposite: Hughie Hughes (euphonium) was a volunteer member of the lifeboat crew for 22 years, following in the footsteps of his grandfather, another George Brookes (who could not swim!). With the 'Lilly Wainwright' are (left to right): George Scarth (RNLI supporter and benefactor), Meurig Davies (coxswain), Tony Frost (2nd coxswain), David Noakes, Bryn Jones, Hughie Hughes, Gordon Short, Ian McNeill, Robert Smith, Glyn Chambers, and John Roberts 'Tan Wal'. (Photo: RNLI) often joined with John J. Edwards, John Holmes and John Ridler to provide the fanfares for the annual inauguration of Crown Court judges at Caernarfon Crown Courts. However, this quiet revolution hardly swamped the Band with female players overnight; for several years the only girls who joined were brought along by their fathers - Miss Julie Edwards (daughter of John J.) and Miss Ruth Shaw (daughter of Walter) who came along with her brother Ian.

But in the late 1960s it was still a novelty to see ladies in a band. In 1970, the annual North Wales Brass Band Association autumn contest was held at Llandudno, and a newspaper report on the event draws attention to the fact that 'the musicians included several young boys and many young women. Rhyl Silver Band, for example, included six young women'. Rhyl were amongst the prizes in both March and Selection categories at the contest, but on this occasion Llandudno Town Band carried off the First Prize in the senior Selection competition, and the Second Prize in the March category.

As Popular as Ever

The shows on the promenade carried on through the 1960s and into the 1970s. The talent competitions were as popular as ever. David A. Jones would spend the whole evening behind the bandstand, taking the names of competitors and organising the music they wished to sing. There were usually far more volunteers than could be accommodated in an evening, especially for the children's competitions. When one young lad was turned away, allegedly for the third evening running, his furious mother belaboured John J. Edwards with her handbag! It is estimated that over 4,000 Glamorous Grandmothers took part in the Friday night competitions over the years.

A thought must be spared again for the hard-working deckchair assistants, who at this time were putting out and collecting between 1,000 and 1,500 chairs a night. The crowds used to gather to watch the amazingly efficient way they worked before and after the shows. On one occasion, Tom Francis Jones and Alan Jones

A Poem received at Llandudno Town Hall

Now, here at Llandudno, they have a Town Band
Who play on the Prom every evening – they're grand.
All stalwart musicians, they blow good and hard,
Conducted by Robin – a bit of a card!

They've been here for years, giving pleasure to all,
Outliving theatre, concert parties and all;
They do a grand job seven evenings a week,
Conducted by Robin – that lad's full of cheek!

On Sundays the crowd do their hymn-singing best;
We go through the hymn-sheet, we're put to the test.
Calon Lan's a winner with all the Welsh folk,
Conducted by Robin – but not as a joke.

During the week, competition's the thing; you
Can conduct the Band, tell a joke, even sing;
It's all in good spirit and loads of good fun,
Conducted by Robin – that lad takes the bun!

Your holiday's over, you have to leave Wales;
You're laughing at photos, remembering tales
That you heard in Llandudno; your time there was grand.
Our thanks to Robin and Llandudno Town Band!

By Albert Shaw of Manchester, 6th August 1970

On 1st July 1969 HRH Prince Charles was invested as 21st Prince of Wales at Caernarfon Castle. In Llandudno, the whole town celebrated with an elaborate pageant at the North Wales Theatre (now Venue Cymru), which did not end until 2am the next day. The Town Band appeared as "The Soldiers of the Queen". (Photo: Jean Lomas)

literally 'went for the record' – the band correspondent of the Daily Herald set them a target of putting down 200 chairs in 3 minutes, which they achieved, and as far as we know it has never been surpassed. Of course, the real reason they became so quick about their task was to enable them to get to the pub after the show!

But despite good attendances the 1960s' balance sheets showed a loss in every year except 1964. In 1965, after a particularly wet season, the bandsmen could only be paid by borrowing from the separately-held Instrument Fund. This was unfortunate as, by 1967, the state of some of the Band's instruments was giving cause for concern. Playing every night for five months of the year really takes its toll on the valve pistons, never mind all the dents and scratches picked up along the way. Some of the basses had been in use since 1923! Accordingly, agreement was reached with the

Council (the Trustee of the Band's instruments) to replace all 25 instruments at a cost of £3,250, the Council contributing £2,000.

This was the first time the Band had had a full set of instruments built in 'Low Pitch'. In May 1939, tuning pitch was standardised to A = 440Hz; before then, instruments were made slightly shorter (High Pitch), and a band having a mixture of older High Pitch and modern Low Pitch instruments often had difficulty playing in tune. Now the Band was fully up to date and standardised.

The following year the uniforms had to be replaced, again with help from the Council. The price of deckchairs had to be increased, but so did the pay of the bandsmen and the deckchair team. In 1969 the loss amounted to £738 and the players' bonuses had to be reduced.

But the playing standard of the Band was still impressive. In 1971 the Band swept the board at the North Wales Brass Band Association Rally at Rhyl in November, winning the association cup and the president's trophy for Best Selection and Best March. They were once again trained and conducted on the day by Mr Reg Little, while Robin Williams acted as compere for the competition.

Robin Williams Retires

At last, in 1972, Robin Williams decided it was time to retire from the conductorship. He was now almost seventy years of age and had been a member of the Band for sixty. He remained as secretary and treasurer, though, until his full retirement from Council employment in 1975. There were many tributes to his long and popular career, and many regular visitors to the resort will have missed his nightly appearances on the promenade. He was the life and soul of Llandudno's evening entertainment for over twenty years, and his contribution to the popularity and success of the resort cannot be overstated. He passed away in 1985.

In April 1976 Mr Jack Beardmore (left) resigned his post as conductor, at the same time as Mr George Brookes left to take over as bandmaster of Conwy Band. Llandudno Band was without a regular musical director for several years.

Mr Jack Beardmore

The post of bandmaster and musical director was now taken by Mr Jack Beardmore, a former cornet player with the Royal Marines Portsmouth Band. He was originally from Manchester, and had started to play the cornet with the Stretford Old Prize Band when he was ten years old. During his Marines' career he studied conducting under Sir Vivien Dunn, and he served a posting as the principal cornet on the Royal Yacht 'Britannia'. Before coming to Llandudno he lived in south Caernarfonshire and was bandmaster of the re-formed Nantlle Vale Silver Band. He was now working as a brass tutor in Gwynedd schools, and lived in the Craig y Don area of Llandudno.

As a former military man, Mr Beardmore was well used to turning out smartly on parade. A new bandmaster's uniform was ordered for him, and he proudly wore it for the first time at a concert in front of the Town Hall. Unfortunately, as he raised his baton to commence the concert, a passing seagull did what seagulls do, and lavishly decorated both cap and tunic. Mr Beardmore did not appreciate either the extra 'scrambled egg' or the bandsmen's laughter!

Mr Beardmore's experience as a naval bandsman also stood him in good stead on the occasions when certain cruise ships visited the resort. For several years, the American MS '*Kungsholm*' called at Llandudno, and her passengers were greeted by the Town Band as they disembarked on to the pier for a day in the town. She was followed in 1975 by her sister-ship MS '*Gripsholm*' on her world cruise.

1974 saw the retirement of one of the Band's stalwarts – Reg O. Williams, trombonist. He had been in the Band almost long enough to remember it as the St Tudno Silver Band, joining as one of Mr Traversi's original junior learners in 1912.

In 1975 Her Majesty the Queen visited Bangor as part of the Cathedral's centenary celebrations. The Band played a fanfare, specially composed by George Brookes, and this was played repeatedly on the television over the coverage of the event.

Mr Beardmore carried on the promenade performances and talent shows for four seasons, and was unfortunate enough to preside at one of the Band's darkest moments. On one evening in 1975 a gentleman was giving his rendition of 'Maybe it's because I'm a Londoner' when he abruptly collapsed on the stage. Members of the Band came to his assistance, but he had suffered a heart-attack and died before the ambulance arrived. The band secretary Mr Tom Owen helped to comfort his distressed wife, and sent an appropriate tribute to the funeral, but the incident cast a shadow over the nightly shows for some time.

In April 1976 Mr Beardmore resigned from the post of bandmaster. He had not been well the previous season and George Brookes had deputised for him several times. However, Mr Brookes had now taken up the position of bandmaster with the nearby Conwy Band, so once again advertisements were placed in the band press for a musical director. In late 1976 the post was offered to composer and band director Mr Gordon Kitto from Durham. He was very keen to take the job, and his two cornet-playing sons were looking forward to joining the Band. The Band Committee asked the Council for help in finding Mr Kitto some daytime employment, but nothing was forthcoming and Mr Kitto never came to Llandudno.

The secretary's post was now taken by Mr G. N. Taylor, but it proved impossible to find a permanent musical director. The 1977 promenade season was conducted by the Band's long-serving cornet player, Bill Jones. This year also saw the Queen's Silver Jubilee celebrations and Her Majesty's visit to Llandudno on Wednesday 22nd June. In the August, Mr Frank Boylin of Old Colwyn was appointed, but he only stayed for the rest of that year.

But the following year more trouble came from a quite unexpected quarter, and a dispute arose which caused not only radical changes, but even threatened the Band's very survival.

Mr Bill Jones directs the Town Band and is introduced to Her Majesty the Queen during her Silver Jubilee visit to Llandudno on 22nd June, 1977.

Chapter 9

Changing Times, 1978-2002

1978 – The Watershed Year

All this time the Llandudno Urban District Council, and its successor the Llandudno Town Council, had supported the Band in many ways: through the annual grant, which had risen steadily over the decades; through the provision of the rehearsal room above the old fire station; through loans and grants for the bandmaster's salary, instruments and uniforms; through the construction and maintenance of the bandstand, and provision of the promenade deckchairs. In return, Llandudno had a famous seaside band which attracted thousands of visitors to the resort and provided music for civic occasions, as required. The relationship between Band and Council had always been, therefore, generally harmonious.

But in April 1978 all this changed. As usual, rehearsals were under way for the summer season, conducted again by Bill Jones, but it became known that the deckchairs would not be ready in time for the beginning of the season. A difference of opinion arose, as to whether the Band should perform without the chairs (and the income they provided) - the outcome was that the Band again found itself without a conductor.

The financial state of the Band was also giving the Town Councillors cause for serious concern. By now the Band was simply costing too much to run, and they were not prepared to finance the deficit any longer. By June it was looking as though the Llandudno Band would not be available for the summer season at all, and arrangements were made with Conwy Band to cover the Mayoral Sunday procession and Remembrance Sunday.

Running concurrently with this dispute was another issue:

The cornet section of the Band playing the Last Post at the Cenotaph on the promenade on a wet Remembrance Day: left to right, John Hughes, Ian Shaw, John Holmes, John Ridler and George Brookes. The Band has provided this service to the Royal British Legion every year except one: 1978, when the Band was temporarily suspended.

The Willie Weis Oompah Band, featuring members of the Town Band: John Ridler, Brian Ashton, John Holmes, Geoff Eschle, John J. Edwards, Frank Ash and Bill Jones. After the dispute with the Council, the oompah band bought their own instruments and, with their promenade commitment reduced, took on engagements as far afield as Lancashire. They even made a short trip to Oman.

some members of the Band were also playing in a German beer-band they had formed the year before. The Willie Weis Oompah-Band turned out for fun evenings in local hostelries, donating some of their earnings to charities but also making a few pounds for themselves. Without a second thought, they used their Band instruments and rehearsed in the bandroom.

There were, however, some members of the Council who considered that the oompah-band was a separate entity and had no right to use the Band's facilities, and thus the Town Band had flouted the terms of their contract. So it was that the Town Band arrived for rehearsal one evening to find that the lock on the bandroom door had been changed and they could no longer get in.

Hughie Hughes (euphonium and bass drum) was determined that the Band should not close down, and made arrangements to rehearse at the Royal Air Force Association Club in Madoc Street. But despite the appointment of another new conductor, Mr Don Mounfield, attendance at rehearsals fell to scarcely a dozen players. In August the decision was taken to disband temporarily, and letters were sent to all members asking for their instruments and uniforms to be handed in.

By October, feelings had cooled and steps were taken to reconcile the two sides. Representatives of the Band met with Councillors, all aired their grievances and then decided to work together again as before. The Band would be re-formed and welcomed back and the grants would be reinstated. But it was decided that it was no longer possible to pay the bandsmen a premium for their appearances, and, consequently, they could not be expected to attend on seven nights out of seven. Promenade concerts would be reduced to three per week, plus hymn-singing on Sundays. The talent shows were abandoned; indeed, they had never been quite so successful without the showman Robin Williams, and most musical directors were far more comfortable preparing and performing band music rather then compering for Glamorous Grannies.

The Band was re-formed in the autumn of 1978, and appointed Mr Robert D. Morgan from Blaenau Ffestiniog as musical director. He was a peripatetic brass tutor for Gwynedd schools and the conductor of the Royal Oakeley Band. He led the Band for two seasons, but found that his Band and school commitments were incompatible. He was succeeded in January 1981 by George H. Brookes, who returned to Llandudno after five years as bandmaster of Conwy Band.

George H. Brookes Returns

Mr Brookes had enjoyed success with Conwy Band, leading them to contest victories on several occasions. He now turned his attention to strengthening the Llandudno Town Band after its recent troubles. As ever he devoted countless hours to training

Over the years the Band has followed the example of Mr Traversi in maintaining a training band for junior players. George Brookes took on the responsibility from an early age, and while he was at Conwy Band Roy Williams took over the role. The young musicians in this photograph are, left to right: Brian Geeson, Russell Dowell, Keith Gibson, Graham Heritage, Suzanne Brookes, and Christopher Short. (Photo: Terry Taylor)

*Crowds and Band fill the promenade for the dedication and naming
ceremony of Llandudno's new Oakley-class lifeboat, the 'Lilly Wainwright',
on 15th May 1964. During her Llandudno career 1964-1990 she assisted in
several high-profile rescues, including the pleasure steamer 'St Trillo' in 1968
and the yacht 'Dyllys' in 1977. The Llandudno lifeboats are provided by the
Royal National Lifeboat Institution and are manned by volunteers.*
www.rnli.org.uk (Photo: John Lawson Reay)

youngsters in both instrumental skills and band musicianship. Under his leadership the Band continued to provide music four nights a week on the promenade, music for civic occasions such as Remembrance Day, and for many other local events. He was

Thomas George Brookes' exceptionally long service with the Band was honoured by his colleagues in 1985, with gifts and a presentation of the 1936 Band poster. At that time Mr Brookes had been with the Band for 63 years, starting as a programme seller in 1922 and then playing flugel and tenor horn. He was still an active Band musician when he passed away in 1995. Back row L to R: George T. Brookes, John Holmes, John Hughes (brother of Griff), Griff Hughes, Ken Roberts, Hugh Hughes, Walter Shaw, David A. Jones, John Ridler, Ian Shaw, John Hughes; Front row: Peter Wareham, George H. Brookes, Thomas G. Brookes, Julie Edwards, John J. Edwards, Bill Jones. (Photo: Baxter's Photography)

Photograph opposite: Hughie Hughes (euphonium) was a volunteer member of the lifeboat crew for 22 years, following in the footsteps of his grandfather, another George Brookes (who could not swim!). With the 'Lilly Wainwright' are (left to right): George Scarth (RNLI supporter and benefactor), Meurig Davies (coxswain), Tony Frost (2nd coxswain), David Noakes, Bryn Jones, Hughie Hughes, Gordon Short, Ian McNeill, Robert Smith, Glyn Chambers, and John Roberts 'Tan Wal'. (Photo: RNLI) ably assisted by David A. Jones (bass trombone), who had returned to the Band after a ten-year absence and was now the secretary and treasurer. Long-standing members John J. Edwards, John Holmes, Hughie Hughes and Walter Shaw also served on the Band Committee.

The End of the Bandroom
In January 1992 Mr Brookes decided to resign as musical director, but continued to act as bandmaster and tutor of the learners' band. At the same time, the Band found itself in danger of having no rehearsal room; the old fire station, and the bandroom above it, were scheduled for demolition.

The fire station had been built on Market Street, at the back of the Council Yard, in 1877, and the Band had used one of its upper rooms as a rehearsal room since 1910. Despite the aforementioned

The junior band standing in front of the old fire station. A room on the first floor had been used as the bandroom since 1910, accessed by means of the open wooden staircase on the outside of the building. Along with other Council properties in the vicinity the fire station was scheduled for demolition in 1992.

post-war rewiring it was always cold and barely adequate as a headquarters. Every summer evening for all those years the Band members had lugged all their instruments and huge piles of music books up and down a rickety external wooden staircase that would have given modern Health and Safety Officers nightmares. When the fire brigade received an emergency telephone call during Band rehearsal, a bell would sound in the practice-room and the music had to stop immediately, so that the officer downstairs could hear the details on the phone. This was also the cue for most of the Band to light up their cigarettes! The fire brigade had moved out in 1970 and although the lower floor had housed the street lighting department for twenty years, parts of it were almost derelict, and a neighbour's bush was growing in through a skylight! The building was well overdue for demolition, but the Band needed another home.

After negotiations with the Council, the former Wages Office at the rear of the Town Hall was made available and fitted with an external door, so that it could be accessed by the Band out of working hours. The room was very small, scarcely able to accommodate a full band, but had to suffice for the time being. The Band made a hurried move out of the old bandroom, barely having time to retrieve all their equipment before the building was demolished. Luckily, someone had the presence of mind to save a tatty box of old Band paperwork.

The conductor's baton passed to Mr Neil Oliver from Holywell, who was a bass player with the Roberts Bakery Band. Unfortunately, he found band life in Llandudno not to his taste, and left after only three months. Further advertisements led to the appointment of Mr James A. Roberts as musical director.

James A. Roberts

'Jim' Roberts was well-known in both Llandudno and the brass band world. He was a local police constable and a Councillor. His musical career had started in the Royal Oakeley Band at Blaenau Ffestiniog, where he had been the principal euphonium player for

In 1992 George Brookes handed over the baton to Mr Jim Roberts, euphonium player and formerly bandmaster of Conwy Band. Mr Brookes is seen here congratulating Mr Roberts on his inauguration as Mayor of Llandudno in 1998.

several years. During his police career he had been stationed in various parts of North Wales, and had played in bands such as Bala Silver, Deudraeth Silver, Royal Nantlle Vale, Rhyl Silver, Trefor, and Nefyn and District. He had been a player in Conwy Town Band during Mr Brookes' time as bandmaster, and had succeeded him in that role in 1981. He was due to retire from the police force in 1993, and so felt able to devote his time to leading the Llandudno Band.

Mr Roberts was bandmaster for six years, from 1992 to 1998. During that time, the difficulties of running an amateur brass band became more apparent. The steady growth of alternative entertainments such as recorded music and television during the 1960s and 70s had not noticeably affected the Band membership while there was the incentive of payment for the players. But, now that the payments had ceased, there was less attraction in working to achieve proficiency on an instrument and in turning out three or four times a week to perform or rehearse. A steady core of players continued as before, but others preferred to pursue different hobbies and entertainments. Somehow, much of the middle of the Band melted away. In several years the age-profile of the Band members showed a polarisation – a large number of juniors and learners, thanks to the tireless efforts of Mr Brookes, a handful of players over 60 years and only one or two in between. The learner-biased ability level and haphazard attendances made it very difficult for the conductor to rehearse effectively, or even find appropriate music that all could enjoy playing.

Recruitment drives were held frequently, through newspaper advertisements and local radio. One of the presenters on Marcher Sound Radio, Mr Ian Turner, was challenged to learn to play a tune on a cornet within a week (he managed 'Twinkle, Twinkle, Little Star'), and this provided good publicity. Other musicians joined and the learners continued to improve. The Band was able to carry out its usual promenade and parade commitments and still achieve thirds and fourths in the NWBBA contests. But just as the situation was getting better the principal cornet, Wesley Heath, left to go to university, the principal trombone John Turner joined the army, and the second trombone's employment took him away from the area. The vacancies remained unfilled for some time.

Another sad loss to the Band was the passing of Thomas George Brookes in December 1995. He had been a member of the Band since he joined as a learner in 1922. He had thus served 73 years as a flugel and tenor horn player, a record of dedication unequalled even in the history of a Band defined by the faithful service of its musicians.

But the Band was still in good heart, and there was much to enjoy. At Easter 1997 Mr Roberts and George Brookes led the Band on a tour to Llandudno's twin town, Wormhout, near Dunkirk in the north of France. The visit mixed solemn ceremonial at local war memorials with more light-hearted entertainments on the town bandstand. Later that year Mr Roberts coached the Band to

Mr George Brookes conducts the Band on the town bandstand in Wormhout, Llandudno's twin town.

second place in the NWBBA contest. Also, like many bands up and down the country, Llandudno Band applied for and was awarded a National Lottery grant towards the cost of a new set of instruments. Although this was, naturally, a cause for celebration, it also caused a few headaches – there was simply not room in the tiny bandroom for all the players and their cases, and the percussion section never had the space to set up their instruments in comfort.

Mr Roberts found himself the butt of a practical joke in 1997 when celebrity chef Ainsley Harriott staged a surprise birthday party for him, as part of a series of programmes celebrating local personalities. The event was organised in great secrecy with the help of Mrs Cynthia Williams, whose son John Wyn played in the Band. Mr Roberts thought he was conducting an ordinary concert at the Lewis Carroll monument at West Shore, and was puzzled when he was required to wear a Tweedle-Dum costume for the occasion. He was even more confused when he was taken to the promenade by Ainsley Harriott, dressed as The Mad Hatter, and found Llandudno and Conwy Bands dressed as playing cards. The world-famous Brighouse and Rastrick Band was assembled on the bandstand and he had the pleasure of conducting them, while renowned cook Marguerite Patten prepared a fabulous display of cakes. Unfortunately the weather took a turn for the worse and everyone, and the cakes, got thoroughly soaked!

"Curiouser and curiouser – why would I need to wear this outfit for a Band concert?" Jim Roberts was completely taken in by Mad Hatter Ainsley Harriott when a special surprise birthday party was organised for him on the promenade.

Mr Roberts became Mayor of Llandudno in 1998, but found that his mayoral and Council commitments left him increasingly unable to devote sufficient time to the Band. Mr Brookes had to deputise for him on numerous occasions. In August 1998 Mr Roberts resigned as musical director and his post was taken on 1st October by Mr Michael D. Jones.

Michael D. Jones

Mr Michael D. Jones was from Beaumaris and had been a cornet player from the age of nine. He had played principal cornet with Beaumaris Band, Gwynedd Schools Brass and Wind bands, the National Youth Brass Band of Wales and the Salford University Brass Band. He then joined the Championship-section Yorkshire Building Society Band, under Mr David King, before returning to

From 1999 to 2002 the Musical Director was Mr Michael D. Jones, who took the Band to a creditable third place at the 1999 National Eisteddfod in Anglesey.

Wales and taking up the post of principal cornet with the Point of Ayr Band. In 1998 he was in his early twenties and felt ready embark on a conducting career to complement his already extensive playing experience.

Coming from the world of Championship-section bands, Mr Jones was keen involve the Band in more competitions, as the intensive rehearsals necessary to prepare a test-piece improve players' technique and raise the standard of their ensemble playing. After only two months in charge Mr Jones led the Band to the annual NWBBA contest at Ysgol John Bright in Llandudno and won first prizes in both the March and Selection categories. The Band also entered the Entertainment Contest at the 1999 Rhyl Festival of Brass, in which it was placed sixth.

Taking part in band contests was a familiar activity to a player of such experience, but the other side of Llandudno Town Band's life, the annual summer season on the promenade, presented a new challenge to Mr Jones. He admitted to being 'daunted' by the prospect of compering the shows, but was soon into the swing of things. He sometimes played cornet solos himself during the programmes. David Constantine's poem 'The Llandudno Town Band' clearly describes a promenade concert of this period (see page 130).

Mr Jones continued his pursuit of competition success at the 1999 National Eisteddfod in Anglesey, and commented afterwards that their third place might have been improved upon with a full complement of players, better attendance at rehearsals, and more private practice by individuals. He also referred to the lack of room in the bandroom: 'These last two months ...we had the second and third cornets cowering under their chairs because the cymbals and timpani were being beaten right next to their heads.' Efforts continued in earnest to find another practice room, but in vain.

This being the era of a great increase in the use of technology, rehearsals at this time were often interrupted by the sound of the younger members' mobile phones alerting them to the arrival of a text message. This was understandably annoying for Mr Jones and other players, and the Band Committee decided to put a stop to it. Accordingly, John J. Edwards announced one evening that mobile phones must be switched to 'silent' during rehearsals, and the junior members obediently turned off their devices. Later the same evening, a mobile phone rang during the practice; there was a frantic hunt for the offending article, which was eventually found ... in John Edwards' pocket. Sheepishly he admitted he did not know how to turn it off!

In 2001, Mr Jones was delighted to be able to collaborate with local record-producer and Band vice-president Mr Gordon Lorenz to produce the Band's first recording on compact disc. The programme included 'Those Magnificent Men in Their Flying Machines', 'Watching the Wheat' and other typical bandstand fare – it was appropriately entitled 'A Promenade Concert'.

In the autumn of the year 2000, George H. Brookes received official recognition for his many years of selfless service to his Band and the Town of Llandudno when he was appointed as a Member of the Order of the British Empire. He was invested with the MBE at Buckingham Palace by HRH Prince Charles, the Prince of Wales.

HRH Prince Charles officially opened the new St David's Hospice in Llandudno in 1999. (Photo: Baxter's Photography)

By early 2002, Mr Jones' ambition to raise the standard of the Band above the Fourth Section was still unfulfilled. There were the perennial personnel problems, and in spite of players moving to other instruments to fill gaps the shortage of players caused the Band to have to withdraw from more than one contest. Mr Jones found this frustrating and disappointing and it was principally for this reason, but also because he had resumed his playing career, that he resigned from the directorship in February 2002.

Once again there were advertisements and appeals in the press for a new musical director. Mr Brookes again stepped in to keep the promenade concerts going, but he did not wish to fill the post full-time – after all, he was now in his seventies and still coaching the juniors as well. The Band needed someone who could devote time and energy to carry it forward.

George H. Brookes MBE, with his wife Betty, after receiving his honour from HRH The Prince of Wales at Buckingham Palace.

In 2001 Hughie Hughes' years of dedication to the community, as bandsman and lifeboat crew, were honoured when he became a Member of the Order of the British Empire (MBE). At the presentation at Buckingham Palace, HRH Prince Charles the Prince of Wales asked Hughie what he would do if lifeboat duty called while he was playing with the Band? Hughie, with a twinkle in his eye, replied that he would carry on playing – there were more lifeboat-men available than euphonium players!

The Llandudno Town Band
by David Constantine

High water behind them the town band
Give us a tune while the sun goes down
Which it does too soon
Leaving us cold in the lee of the big headland

The old and the very old in stripy deckchairs
Recumbent under wraps like a year ago
And some drawn up alongside in flash new wheelchairs
The same old crowd, minus the passed away,

Huddling together on the big prom
Under the vast sky here we are again:
Sacred on Sundays and the profane
Mondays, Wednesday and Fridays, always at 8 p.m.

Against the surf, under the cackling gulls
What a brave noise they make, it cheers me up no end:
Fatty the Tuba with the very thick spectacles
Ballooning fast, and his lady friend

(I call her his lady friend) blowing him kisses
The length of her brassy trombone
And two very pretty things, sex unknown,
Winking over their cornets in white blouses.

The gulls jeer and a shrewd wind blows
And but for the plastic clothes pegs in nine bright colours
Away would go the tunes from the shows
Like all the other litter of our yesteryears.

To finish, Dave the conductor promises a solo
But doesn't say it's Sally on the flugelhorn
Or Bob on sax and the regulars know
It's him himself and he'll suddenly turn

And it won't be the twiddling stick he'll hold
But the trumpet and there he'll swell
Facing us, full frontal
And such a sound will come forth, pure gold

Out of his silver, and not the Last Post
Nor the Last Trump either though I grant you an angel
Recording on the Orme would think it must
Be Jehoshaphat down here – no, our Dave'll

Close his eyes and deliver what he can hear
In his head or his heart or up there in the sky
And give it us neat, give it us proof and pure
On and on, in and in, till every body

And in every body the huddled soul
Shy as an embryo
Hearkens. Then that's it for now,
That's it till Sunday and *Abide With Me* and all

Not stiff for ever get to their feet
And the wheelchair-riders sit up straight
And the team in purple sound and tinkle the tune
For us to hum *Land of My Fathers* and sing *God Save the Queen*

And we do our best but it's not much cop
Against the whole of the Irish Sea
Come very close. The band pack up,
It's cold, the wheelchairs speed away.

David Constantine, 'Collected Poems' (Bloodaxe Books, 2004)

The Llandudno Town Band in 2002.
Standing, left to right: George Brookes, Geoff Coombes, Flo Jones,
John Ridler, Tim Kinsley, Sarah Hughes, Jonathan Kirkham, David A. Jones,
John J. Edwards, Don Caiger, Allen Hughes, Ken Jones, Walter Shaw,
Hugh Hughes;
Front row: Ruth Coleman Jones, Heulwen Hughes, Robert Rodrigues,
2 cornets (sadly unrecorded), John Hughes, John Wyn Williams,
Thomas Hughes.
(Photo: Weekly News)

Chapter 10

Into the New Century, 2002-2015

Clive E. Wolfendale

2002 passed without any response to the appeals, but in 2003 an article in the North Wales Daily Post drew the attention of Mr Clive E. Wolfendale. A career policeman, he had recently moved to the Llandudno area to take up the post of Assistant Chief Constable with the North Wales Police. Mr Wolfendale had been a clarinet player since the age of nine and had played for over thirty years with the Adamson Military Band in Dukinfield (his home town), east Manchester. He had also played in the Greater Manchester Police Band and for some years had led the Amos Brown dance band in the city. He had been the musical director of the Adamson Band for twelve years, but his move to North Wales had deprived him of his musical activities – now he wanted to get involved again. By his own admission, he often couldn't decide whether policing or music had a greater call on his time. Initially, Mr Wolfendale helped out at Llandudno by taking a few rehearsals and the occasional Prom concert, and then was offered the post of musical director in September 2003.

Clive Wolfendale as Chief Constable of North Wales Police. He joined the Greater Manchester Police in 1975, attracted as much by its excellent military band as the career prospects.
(Photo: S. Wolfendale)

For the first time in its history, Llandudno Town Band was led by a man who was not a brass-bandsman. This should not, of course, make any difference at all to the coaching of the Band – the musical director should not have to instruct players on brass technique, but rather be fashioning a musical performance from the entire ensemble. But Mr Wolfendale's outlook on running a brass band was perhaps slightly different to others who had gone before him; as a result of his previous involvement in a non-competitive community band, his over-riding priority was to make his new Band, true to its roots, a vital part of the Llandudno entertainment scene. Contests were something of a distraction, although enjoyable and beneficial in small doses.

The emphasis, therefore, was on improving the quality of the twice-weekly promenade appearances, and in undertaking more concerts generally. This proved frustrating, initially, due to the constant shortage of players. But Mr Wolfendale introduced some new projects which helped to increase enthusiasm and attract new members. Like Robin Williams many years before, he felt that a brass band needed to move with the times and engage with its audience; he set about updating the Band's library of music, introducing more modern 'pop' tunes and well-known music from the 1960s onwards, to complement the traditional brass band fare.

His first major project was to produce a second recording of the Band on compact disc. Mr Wolfendale was an enthusiastic supporter of Welsh culture and language, and visitors to the bandstand always like to take home a Welsh souvenir, so in 2005, the Band recorded "The Great Orme' – Songs of Wales', which featured an entire programme of Welsh melodies and works by Welsh composers. The recording was made in St John's Methodist Church, Mostyn Street and was produced by Band vice-president and music promoter, Gordon Lorenz.

Whit Friday Band Contests
Another innovation, in 2006, was a trip to the Whit Friday band competitions at Saddleworth, near Oldham (see panel). Mr

Whit Friday Band Competitions in Saddleworth

The Saddleworth band contests developed as a part of the Whit Friday 'Walks of Witness' conducted each year by churches in the Manchester and surrounding areas. This was one of the highlights of the church year, when congregations paraded through their towns and joined together for a communal service. Best clothes were the order of the day, and children might have their only new suit of clothes for the entire year for the occasion. After the service, a carnival atmosphere prevailed, and later in the afternoon and evening the bands that had led the morning's processions played against one another in a quickstep (march) competition.

Over the years, Whit Friday as a religious occasion has declined, whereas the band competitions have expanded beyond their traditional range. Once confined to Saddleworth villages with now-famous names such as Diggle, Delph and Dobcross, the contests have now spread into the neighbouring Tameside area of Manchester. On the Friday evening, the region is criss-crossed by coaches bearing bands from all over the British Isles (and beyond), each trying to compete in as many of the village competitions as possible before darkness makes playing impossible.

Although most bands treat the occasion as a grand day out, there is serious prize money on offer at many venues, and the better bands can end the day with several large cheques. At each venue, the main event is a performance of a march on the podium, judged by a hidden adjudicator who cannot see which band is playing. Prior to this, each band plays a 'street march' as they parade from their bus along the village street, and in some places there is a Deportment prize on offer for the best marching, regardless of what the music sounds like! Bands typically manage to attend between six and ten venues during the evening, depending on traffic and the number of bands queuing to play at each village. Experienced campaigners plan their routes very carefully to maximise their chances and avoid delays.

Part of the attraction of the event is the all-inclusive range of bands who attend; the local youth band may be followed down the street by the world-famous Brighouse and Rastrick Band, or a band from Norway, or even a made-up-for-the-day band of caravan enthusiasts!

Mr Clive Wolfendale concentrates fiercely while conducting the podium march at a Saddleworth Whit Friday contest. In the background, Walter Shaw and Aaron Bisby.

Wolfendale was surprised to find that, in the whole of its nearly-100-year history, Llandudno Band had only participated in this famous brass band event on one or two occasions in Mr Skelton's time. His former band, The Adamson Band, although based close to Saddleworth, was barred because it includes woodwind instruments. So Mr Wolfendale invited the brass players from Adamson's to supplement the Llandudno Band, and the combined ensemble was led along the streets by the Adamson Drum Major and drum corps. At each competition venue, a regulation 25 players were selected to perform the podium march. The combination of disciplined music-making and a good day out immediately made this event an annual favourite, and an added bonus was the award of the Deportment Prize at Stalybridge on three occasions.

Formal contests were not neglected, however, and Llandudno Town Band continued to support the annual NWBBA event each November, bringing home first and second prizes on several occasions. In addition, the Band began to enter the National Eisteddfod competition every alternate year, when the Festival was held in North Wales. Mr Wolfendale saw this as an opportunity to fly the flag for Llandudno, as the competition was always broadcast live on S4C, the Welsh-language television channel. At the Faenol Eisteddfod in 2005 the Band was placed third, playing an all-Welsh programme including Tony Traversi's 'Great Orme' march. In 2007 at Mold they were awarded the third prize, and in 2009 at Bala they won the second prize with 'Singin' In The Rain' and 'Great Western Themes'. S4C also asked Mr Wolfendale to appear on

The great Welsh cultural festival, the National Eisteddfod, is held annually and alternates between venues in the north and the south of the country. Mr Wolfendale took the Band to the competitions at Bala in 2009, Mold in 2007 and, here, Y Faenol near Bangor in 2005.

several occasions as a pundit during the live TV coverage to provide his 'expert' comments on the other bands' performances – a rather harrowing experience for a learner of the Welsh language!

Familiar Faces Leave the Band

Sadly, the time inevitably comes when a bandsman's playing days are over, and several of the Band's musicians had been serving since the 1950s and 60s. In 2005 John Holmes, on his retirement after 35 years as a postman, decided it was also time to retire gracefully from the first tenor horn chair. He had joined the Band as a junior in 1952, when George Brookes had taught him baritone, and he had gone on to play cornet as well as tenor horn.

By 2008 Hughie Hughes was in poor health, but he managed to attend the promenade concerts on his scooter. That Christmas was the first for over fifty years that he did not go out carolling with the Band, nor played Christmas morning carols in the Merrion Hotel. He passed away in March 2009, and his beloved Band played at his moving memorial service in St John's Methodist Church on Mostyn Street.

Church services

In the first years of the 21st century a regular partnership developed between St John's Methodist Church, St David's Methodist Church in Craig y Don and the Band. For a few years the Band had provided music for both churches' carol services at Christmas, but in 2007 was also invited to play the hymns and seasonal music for the Easter service at St David's. At this time both churches were led by the same minister, The Rev'd Nick Sissons, who, like Mr Wolfendale, liked to add a dash of humour to the occasion. The two of them competed gently throughout the services in making jokes at each other's expense, and although Mr Sissons later moved on, becoming the chaplain at nearby Rydal Penrhos School, the special services proved so popular with the congregations that the practice still continues today.

A Night at the Movies

But the principal activity of the Llandudno Town Band remained the promenade entertainment during the summer season. By the early years of the twenty-first century this had reduced to two evenings a week, plus hymns on Sundays. But a succession of poor summers saw the concerts rained off so often that Band morale and commitment was very low, and receipts from audience collections were much reduced.

In 2008 Mr Wolfendale decided to replace one of the weekly promenade performances with an indoor concert, to ensure that the Band played regularly, whatever the weather. This was something of a gamble, as the receipts had to at least cover the hire of the Town Hall and other costs. And would holiday-makers be prepared to come out to a brass band concert? Most of the hotels nowadays provided their own entertainment in-house – there had to be a good incentive for visitors to leave their cosy accommodation on a rainy evening.

Mr Wolfendale put together a programme of well-known film and television music of varying styles, from theme songs, such as 'Everything I Do, I Do It For You', to grand orchestral numbers like 'Gladiator'. Rather than present a staid collection of items in concert format, Mr Wolfendale introduced a comic element by donning an appropriate costume for each piece and engaging in light banter with the audience. Audiences got a bit of a shock at first – it is not normal for the conductor to leave the stage and return wearing a fluorescent jacket and a miner's helmet ('Brassed Off'!) - but soon warmed to the idea and the evenings usually became quite hilarious by the second half.

The 'Film Night' concerts ran for two seasons in the Town Hall, and a large part of the credit for their success must go to second-cornet Mrs Jane Bonser and her husband James, who obtained or made all the costumes, produced a soundtrack quiz to cover the minutes while the conductor was changing costume, and provided the interval refreshments. The concerts gained a popular reputation and it was noticed that members of the audience returned the second year for more. Unfortunately, however, before the third season the balcony area of the Town Hall concert room was closed for safety reasons, and with only the ground floor available for paying seats the concerts became uneconomical to run. Summer entertainment reverted wholly to the promenade.

Mr Wolfendale kept the Band busy with other projects, and produced another compact disc recording in 2009, 'Llandudno Band at the Movies'. He was also aware that 2010 was approaching, the year the Llandudno Town Band would mark its centenary. He intended to celebrate the occasion with as many special events as the Band could accommodate, and bring Llandudno Town Band back into the limelight.

Centenary of the Llandudno Town Band
The question of how to celebrate the centenary had been raised by

John J. Edwards as early as 2007, and planning now began in earnest. The main event would be a gala concert at Llandudno's premier theatre, Venue Cymru, and the attendance of Britain's foremost euphonium soloist Mr David Childs was secured. Celebrated brass band composer Mr Philip Sparke was commissioned to write a celebratory piece of music for the occasion, and funds were provided for the project by the Arts Council of Wales. The Band was invited to Llandudno's twin town of Wormhout, and it was decided that the centenary could not pass without the Band participating in the National Eisteddfod, even though it was being held that year in the south of Wales.

The Band had never experienced quite such an extended period of extraordinary events, which had to be prepared for alongside all the regular activities. The new piece, 'Centennial Salute', arrived, and had to be rehearsed; although composed with a Fourth Section band in mind, it had some difficult passages, with rapid finger-work required from several players. It was decided that it would be fitting to perform it for the first time at the National Eisteddfod, which would be shown live on television. But before that happened, the Band would engage in its short trip to Wormhout.

Wormhout
During the first weekend of July 2010 the Llandudno Town Band travelled again to northern France, along with members of the town's Twinning Committee, various groups of young people from the town, and the Mayor of Llandudno, Councillor Mrs Ann M. Yates. The Band played The Last Post at several war memorial sites in the locality, and presented an engraved flugel-horn at the Wormhout Barn memorial. On the Saturday afternoon the Band participated in the local Esquelbec Literary Festival, and that evening joined with the Wormhout Town Band in an evening entertainment at the town's community centre.

The church in Wormhout has a wonderful acoustic which perfectly suits the sound of a brass band. On the Sunday morning

In Centenary year, the Band was invited to Llandudno's twin town,
Wormhout, in northern France. Llandudno's link with Wormhout dates
from May 1940, when the 69th Medium Regiment of the Caernarvon and
Denbigh Yeomanry, based in Llandudno, found itself out of ammunition and
retreating towards Dunkirk from the advancing German forces in Flanders.
The Germans ambushed the British force at Wormhout and subsequently
massacred their prisoners in a barn at Esquelbec. A few soldiers survived to
tell the world about the atrocity, among them Gunner Richard Parry
from Llandudno.
The Band donated an engraved flugel horn to be displayed in the restored
Memorial Barn, and the trumpeters sounded the Last Post in tribute to the
fallen soldiers.
(Photo: S. Wolfendale)

the Band contributed three solemn items to the Morning Mass, which members of the congregation found very moving. This was followed by both bands marching to a short ceremony at the town memorial. Throughout the visit the Band received a very warm welcome from their fellow musicians and the people of Wormhout.

The combined bands of Llandudno and Wormhout paraded along the main street before a short service at the town memorial.
(Photo: David Greenman)

Centenary Celebrations

Back to Wales, and back to the hard work: evenings on the promenade, and three pieces to prepare for the Eisteddfod. In addition to the world premiere of 'Centennial Salute', the programme would consist of 'Concierto de Aranjuez', featuring flugel soloist Miss Sarah Hughes, and 'It's Not Unusual', the Tom Jones classic, in deference to the Eisteddfod's location at Ebbw Vale in the Welsh Valleys. An early start and a long day on a coach were rewarded with third prize in the competition.

It was shortly after the National Eisteddfod that the Band was delighted to be informed that, in recognition of a century of service to the community, the Llandudno Town Council wished to award the Freedom of the Town to the Llandudno Town Band. The presentation was to be made at the centenary concert.

The Band was also honoured when Lord Mostyn and Mostyn Estates Ltd marked the centenary with a gift of a new drum kit, much appreciated as the old one was suffering from many years' exposure to the sea air.

The Centenary Concert

Preparations for the centenary concert were complicated by the number of performers involved. In addition to Mr Childs, the programme would feature the Maelgwn Male-Voice Choir and baritone vocalist Mr Elgan Llŷr Thomas. Many people think that it is easy to put on a joint concert between two or more musical organisations, but in fact it is complicated by the different needs of the various groups. For example, Mr Thomas wished to sing 'The Music of the Night', from 'The Phantom of the Opera', but was the Band's version of it in the right key for him? If not, the whole set of music would have to be rewritten so that he would not be straining too high or too low. Did the Band have the music to accompany

On behalf of all the Band members, George H. Brookes received the official parchment conferring Honorary Freedom of the Town of Llandudno to the Band. The Mayor of Llandudno Mrs. Ann M. Yates presented the honour during the Band's centenary concert at Venue Cymru on Sunday 12th September 2010.

any items in the Choir's repertoire, and would that be in the right key for them? The Band had obtained the music to accompany Mr Childs' solos, but could they play them well enough for his liking? And would there be any opportunity to get everyone together to rehearse?

In the event, everyone was able to meet up for just one rehearsal on the Friday evening, and the centenary concert took place on the Sunday afternoon, 12th September 2010, conducted by Mr Clive Wolfendale and compered by Mr Dilwyn Roberts. Mr Childs amazed everyone with his dexterity and phenomenal range of styles and effects. The bewildering speed of the virtuoso numbers contrasted brilliantly with his expressive tone in the slow ballads, and his encore, 'The Hot Canary', contained the most un-euphonium-like squeaks. Former Band-member Elgan Llŷr Thomas showed why he is so often an eisteddfod winner and studying at the Royal Northern College of Music, with emotive performances of two Lloyd Webber classics. The Maelgwn Choir added their sonorous harmony to the Band's accompaniment, as

Britain's foremost euphonium soloist, David Childs, performing with the Band at the centenary concert. His programme featured contrasting lyrical and virtuosic numbers: 'Brillante', by Peter Graham; 'Softly as I Leave You', arr. de Vita; 'Lament' by Karl Jenkins; 'My Grandfather's Clock' by George Doughty, and Paul Nero's 'Hot Canary' as an encore. More information at: www.davechilds.com

The Llandudno Town Band in its Centenary year:
Back row, left to right: Joe Roberts, Susan Wolfendale, Lisa Howarth, Jane Bonser, Robert Rodrigues.
Middle row: Dek Pickersgill, Selwyn Price, Ken Hughes, Sonia Jones, John Ridler, Don Caiger, Bethan Oliver-Jones,
David A. Jones, Ken Jones, Emlyn Thomas, John Wyn Williams, John Hughes, Martin Howarth, Victoria Hodgkinson,
Sarah Hughes;
Front row: Barry Cripps, Tim Kinsley, Gwenan Hughes, Alan Peachey, John J. Edwards, Clive E. Wolfendale, George H.
Brookes, Walter Shaw, Allen Hughes, Simon Hughes, George T. Brookes.
(Photo: David Greenman)

Elgan Llŷr Thomas took his first musical steps under the guidance of George Brookes. Firstly on cornet, but later on the bass, Elgan was a member of the Band until he left to continue his vocal studies at the Royal Northern College of Music in Manchester. He is a recipient of a Study Award from the Bryn Terfel Foundation, and has won many prizes at recent National Eisteddfodau. He is currently studying at the Guildhall School of Music and Drama. More information at: www.elganthomas.co.uk

well as performing solo pieces of their own. The performances were enthusiastically received by a large audience and all agreed that the concert had done justice to both the Band and the town.

Appropriately therefore, during the concert Her Worship the Mayor Mrs Ann M. Yates presented to Mr George H. Brookes MBE the official parchment conferring the Freedom of the Town on the Llandudno Town Band – a fitting honour to acknowledge the long dedication and contribution of the Band to the town and people of The Queen of Welsh Resorts.

Farewell to old friends

At the end of the centenary year, the Band members held a celebratory centenary dinner, not only as an appropriate finale to a special twelve months, but also to honour a number of musicians whose lives had been inextricably linked with the Town Band for many years:

– George H. Brookes, who had announced his retirement from the Band after the centenary concert. He had been a talented musician, instrumental tutor and band trainer for 70 years, all but five of which had been spent in his beloved Llandudno Band. Conceivably the Band would not still exist without his efforts over the years, and the number of brass players who owe their skills and musical knowledge to his tuition probably runs well into three figures;

– John J. Edwards, who also retired from the Band at the end of 2010 after a musical career of over 65 years. His contributions over the years as tenor horn player, band trainer and committee member, are also immeasurable;

– Walter Shaw, a comparative newcomer, who joined the Band in 1965. He had spent a large part of that time serving as the Band Librarian, an onerous and largely thankless task, keeping track of thousands of sheets of music. Mr Shaw retired through poor health in 2012, at the age of 85;

– John Ridler, who at that point could only boast 60 years of service on the cornet and bass tuba, although he is still adding to that tally to this day. Through the years he managed to run concurrent careers in the Band, the Town Council and (in his younger days!) a football team;

– David A. Jones, now in his eighties, who was still serving as secretary and treasurer, and had been playing bass trombone since 1944. In May 2012 the Llandudno Town Council presented him with a Certificate of Merit in recognition of over 40 years in local government service as well as his continuing commitment to the Town Band.

A specially-commissioned poem, entitled 'The Champion Quintet', by Clogwyn ap Doged, was read out in their honour.

The Champion Quintet

Twenty Ten's a special year for all in the Town Band;
A hundred years of blowing in Llandudno, fair and grand.
Songs of Praise, and marching proud, and happy sing-along,
A century of playing to the holidaying throng.

A trip to France, a new CD, 'Centennial Salute';
A Venue Cymru gala show with David Childs to boot!
On top of all these special things, there's something better yet;
This year we hail five gradely men, the Champion Quintet.

We'll start with the bandmaster, Mister George Brookes MBE,
He plays the lot, conducts and, if you like, he'll make the tea.
He's coached some fine musicians and he's taught them all he knows;
The freedom of the town he loves is only what it owes.

John Edwards is the solo horn, a man with nerves of steel,
He never cracks a lofty note, nor makes his tenor squeal.
He likes a round of golf or two, and in the nineteenth hole
You'll find him telling lousy jokes to many a tortured soul.

In minist'ring the band books, David Jones has done the most;
He counts up all the pennies and he deals with all the post.
He also plays the bass trombone with all his energy
And likes a trip round Asda finding bargains for his tea.

John Ridler plays the cornet and he used to be the Mayor,
He dresses to the nines to make the local ladies stare.
He likes a glass of wine or two, or three if it's on tap,
So if you want a good night out, then Ridler is the chap.

Number five is Walter Shaw upon the baritone;
He's also the librarian in the bandroom – and at home
Not only on his instrument does Walter pant and puff;
Of trains and traction engines he just cannot get enough.

We'll never see the likes again of such a grand quintet,
Men of brass and substance town and band will ne'er forget.
They've served as many years as there are days in any one;
The finest bandsmen ever; never bettered, never gone.

Clogwyn ap Doged, 2010

With a Little Help from their Friends

After all the hard work and special events of 2010, the following year could have been an anticlimax for the members of the Llandudno Town Band. With only the usual promenade concerts, church services and civic parades in prospect, they might have felt a twinge of nostalgia for the bustle and busyness of centenary year. But early in 2011 their friend and record-producer Mr Gordon Lorenz suggested the Band record another compact disc.

Gordon Lorenz was quite a celebrity in the town. He had worked with many of the great names of popular music, including Shirley Bassey and Charlotte Church, over many decades. Perhaps his greatest claim to fame was in writing and producing the 1980 Number One Christmas hit, 'There's No One Quite like Grandma'.

This time, therefore, the plan was a little more ambitious: to celebrate fifty years of 'modern' popular music, but with a fusion of the brass band sound with modern electrical instruments and vocalists. And where would be a fitting venue for this project? The place where it

Gordon Lorenz produced literally hundreds of recordings during his career, including several with the Town Band. His final project was the Band's recording at Abbey Road Studios in London.
(Photo: Daily Post)

149

The Fab Four? – Adam Wilson (euphonium), Daniel Greenman (cornet),
John Wyn Williams (euphonium) and Joseph Richards (cornet).
(Photo: David Greenman)

Recording under way in the legendary Studio 2, Abbey Road.
(Photo: David Greenman)

If you are going to Abbey Road, you just have to be photographed on the zebra crossing!
(Photo: David Greenman)

all began, so to speak - the famous Studio 2 at Abbey Road in London, where the Beatles had produced many of their greatest songs. It was an opportunity not to be missed, and very early on the morning of Sunday 15th May 2011 the Band boarded their coach for the trip to the capital.

With the images of Lennon and McCartney, Sting and Rolling Stones looking on, the Band recorded classic songs, from The Beatles to Keane, with their guest vocalists Rachel Zona Chan, Roz Royale, Steve Millington and Matty Roberts. The resulting compact disc, 'Llandudno Town Band at Abbey Road', is a delightful fusion of modern and traditional sounds.

Unfortunately, only a few weeks after the studio visit, Gordon Lorenz died suddenly at his home in Llandudno, leaving the project unfinished. Mr Wolfendale managed to retrieve the master tapes which had been given to engineer Steve Millington to mix. Steve, an accomplished multi-instrumentalist, was also a member of the popular Houghton Weavers folk group. Conductor and engineer worked to bring Gordon Lorenz's dream to fruition. The two can be heard on the arrangement of 'Baker Street' in which Steve Millington's vocal is accompanied by Mr Wolfendale playing the iconic saxophone solo. It is perhaps fitting that, after a career spent producing a prodigious quantity of recordings for many artists, Gordon Lorenz's final work was for the Band of his home town.

Welsh artist Marc Rees likes to provoke thought as well as pleasure through his imaginative installations in and around the town. In July 2012 he brought the display 'Adain Avion' to Llandudno – a complete aeroplane fuselage which spent a week as an exhibition and performance space on the promenade. The plane made a triumphant progress along the prom, towed by members of the public, with the Band playing a specially-commissioned 'Adain Avion' anthem. In subsequent years the Town Band and the Swing Band collaborated again with Marc Rees and Mostyn Estates Ltd on his 'Llawn' series of arts festivals, which featured open-air screenings of the films 'Jaws' and 'Grease'.
(Photo: Roj Smith)

Branching out

The Band continued, as ever, to play during the summer on the promenade bandstand, enjoying some wonderful balmy evenings and dodging showers on other occasions. But some difficulties

A century on from the horrors of the Great War, the Band led the town's memorial parade in August 2014.
(Photo: David Greenman)

were experienced now that so many of the senior players had left, and some of the younger ones went off to university. Mr Wolfendale wondered whether it would be possible to take some performance burden away from the brass band and to give opportunities to local woodwind players. No wind or military bands now existed in the area, even though a century earlier they had been as prevalent as their brass cousins. Accordingly, an article was placed in the local newspaper, inviting woodwind players to come along for an exploratory rehearsal

There was an unexpectedly high level of interest in the project at first, with so many clarinets, flutes and saxophones attending that there were thoughts of expanding into a symphonic wind band. But several of the players had travelled a fair distance from various parts of North Wales, and it soon became clear that a high turnout would not be achieved on a regular basis. However, a small core of saxophone players was keen to form another ensemble, and in late 2012 the Llandudno Swing Band was born. Recreating the sound of the swing era, the group soon became a popular feature at local dances and events such as the Llandudno Air Show and Colwyn Bay 1940s Festival.

Looking to the future

Another development, in the interests of strengthening the Band, was the development of a thriving learners' section. Messrs Traversi and Brookes had always maintained a vibrant training programme for young musicians, some of whom subsequently became the backbone of the Band. This task had become harder in recent years with the advent of so many distractions for young people both in the home and at school. The acquisition of instrumental skills takes hundreds of hours of practice and there are many easier sources of recreation in the twenty-first century. The challenge was taken on by baritone player Sue Hughes, a music graduate of Bangor University and peripatetic teacher. Accommodating players of all ages and standards she established a weekly training rehearsal which gradually attracted a large contingent. The group would occasionally perform in their own right in schools and other social centres.

A New Team

Clive Wolfendale had retired from policing in 2009 after 34 years in the service and in the rank of Chief Constable of North Wales Police. He immediately took up the position of chief executive of CAIS, a Llandudno-based charity providing support services across North Wales to people with drug and alcohol problems. Despite the burden of his new role, Mr Wolfendale continued to juggle the demands of work and music, supported by his wife Susan, and son Richard, who formed the Band's percussion team. In the years after Mr Wolfendale's appointment the work of CAIS expanded both in scope and territory and his responsibilities extended across Wales. Reluctantly, in the spring of 2014 he announced that the summer promenade season would have to be his last.

At this time the secretary and treasurer, David A. Jones, finally relinquished the offices he had discharged diligently for so many years, prior to retiring from playing at the end of 2014. A new generation of administrators stepped into the substantial gap. Mrs Angharad Sherrington (tenor horn) was elected secretary; Mrs Bethan Oliver-Jones (trombone), who had taken over the treasurer's role, was joined by her husband Mr David Jones (euphonium, and brother of former conductor, Michael), who took on the position of bandmaster. In the course of searching for a new conductor the availability of Mr Jim Roberts was established and he returned to the Band in the autumn of 2014.

In Conclusion

It is a remarkable fact that in the 104 year history of the Llandudno Town Band the number of resident conductors barely runs into double figures. There can be few bands with such a record. This continuity of commitment is testament to the status of the Band within the town, the delight of making music in Llandudno, but mostly to the loyalty and comradeship of the players. At a time when institutions, public and voluntary, experience a churn of leadership and standing, this surely points to the pivotal role of the Band in Llandudno and its immense contribution to the town over the past century; The Queen of Welsh resorts with her Handsome Prince of brass bands.

And the Band still does what it has always done...
(Photo: David Greenman)

Players of the Llandudno Town Band

Disclaimer: This list has been compiled from attendance records, photographs and memories covering over 100 years. The attendance records are not complete for all years and ceased when the Bandsmen were no longer paid for their services. Memories are also fallible; there will be unintentional omissions and inaccuracies, for which the author apologises. The List of Players will be published on the Band's website (www.lltb.co.uk), where amendments can be made by contacting the website administrator.

Ash, Frank	Drums	
Bailey, Neil	Cornet	2009-10
Banister, F M		1940
Bather, Andrew	Trombone	1974-80
Baxter, Joseph	Drums	1928
Beardmore, Jack	Bandmaster	1972-75
Bent, Peter	Bass	2006
Bibby, Gordon	Bass	1972-80
Bisby, Aaron J	Euphonium	1999-2004
Bonser, Kelly	Cornet	2006
Bonser, Jane	Cornet	2007-
Boole, Johnny	Horn	1940-42
Boyle, Terry B	Bass	1967-74
Boylin, Frank	Musical Director	1977
Bragg, James	Drums	1993-98
Breeze, Basil S	Baritone	1941-43
Brookes, Thomas George	Cornet/horn	1923-95
Brookes, George Henry (son of T G Brookes)	Cornet/euphonium	1940-2010
Brookes, Arthur (son of T G Brookes)	Euphonium	1954-61
Brookes, Stan (nephew of T G Brookes)	Bass	1954-65
Brookes, Suzanne (dtr of G H Brookes)	Baritone	1970-77

Name	Instrument	Years
Brookes, George T (son of G H Brookes)	Bass	1971-2012
Brownhill, G T		1946
Butler, Steff	Cornet	2005
Caiger, Don	Trombone	1996-2011
Chan, Rachel Zona	Vocalist	2010-11
Coleman Jones, Edward	Trombone	2000-03
Coleman Jones (Shaw), Ruth (daughter of Walter Shaw)	Cornet	1973-
Comton, G		1944
Cripps, Barry	Bass	2007-2010
Davies, Edwin	Horn	1912
Davies, Humphrey	Cornet	1912-13
Davies, Henry	Horn	1937-40
Davies, Edward	Bass	1961-75
Davies, Robert John	Cornet/horn/trombone	1911-37
Davies, J Glyn	Cornet	1937-52
Dawson, Brian	Drums	2000-07
Eccles, Tony	Bass	1968
Edwards, Alan (son of Harry Edwards)	Cornet	1960
Edwards, Arthur Samuel	Euphonium/trombone	1911-23
Edwards, H		1911
Edwards, Harry	Euph/trombone	1925-40
Edwards, J E	Cornet	1911-12
Edwards, Jack W	Cornet/baritone/euph/bass	1912-23
Edwards, John		1941-42
Edwards, John Henry (son of Harry Edwards)	Trombone/organ	1960-65
Edwards, John J	Horn	1949-2010
Edwards, Jack (Salem)	Cornet	1911-24
Edwards, R		1965-68
Edwards, R J	Cornet/soprano/horn	1914-35
Edwards, Robert (1)	Trombone	1911-19
Edwards, Robert (2)	Cornet	1913
Edwards, Sam	Bass	1911-12
Edwards, Sidney Albert	Soprano/cornet/flugel	1912-15

Edwards, Simon	Drums	
Edwards, Susan		
(dtr of John J Edwards)	Horn	1971-78
Edwards (Walker), Julie		
(dtr of John J Edwards)	Horn	1971-82
Etheridge (Pendleton), Julia	Cornet	1965-75
Evans, Ivor	Cornet/baritone	1911-54
Evans, Ll (Clifton Rd)		1911
Evans, Llewelyn (King St/ Ettrick Villa?)		
	Flugel/trombone/bass	1911-26
Evans, Llewelyn J	Bass	1911-14
Evans, R H	Cornet/trombone	1934-37
Evans, Renne	Cornet	1999-2002
Evans, William	Trombone	1921-30
Foulkes, Robert	Cornet/horn	1914-17
Foulkes, William	Cornet/bass	1912-13
Gaskell, Stuart	Bass	2005
Green, Charlotte	Cornet	2011
Greenman, Daniel	Cornet	2009-14
Griffiths, Peter K	Cornet	1979-80
Griffiths, Philip	Trombone/drum	1995-2007
Grundy, James M	Horn/baritone	1943-75
Haf, Elliw	Horn	2011
Haslam, Ian	Horn	1979
Haslam, Mark	Euphonium	1979
Haslock, Mark	Cornet	1979
Heath, Hayley	Cornet	1996-2002
Heath, Wesley	Cornet	1993-2000
Herd, Andrew	Trombone	1975-80
Heritage, Graham	Horn	1979-80
Hingley, Arthur	Trombone/euph	1941-54
Hodgkinson, Victoria	Cornet	2009-10
Holland, Robert J 'Bobby'	Cornet/horn	1926-72
Holland, Thomas George	Euph	1926-40
Holmes, John W	Horn/baritone	1952-2005
Holmes, Paul		
(son of John W Holmes)	Cornet	1982-85

Howarth, Martin	Soprano/cornet/drums	2005-
Howarth, Nick	Drums	2011
Howarth (Smith), Lisa	Percussion	2005-
Hughes, Allen	Baritone	2003-
Hughes, David		
(nephew of T G Brookes)	Euphonium	1942-47
Hughes, Douglas		
(son of John Hughes (2))	Horn	1980
Hughes, G O	Trombone	1930-34
Hughes, Griffith 'Griff'		
(nephew of T G Brookes)	Trombone	1941-80
Hughes, Gwenan	Horn	2009-2012
Hughes, Heardley		1944-47
Hughes, Heulwen		
(sister of Thomas Hughes)	Cornet	1999-2003
Hughes, Hugh		
(nephew of T G Brookes)	Euphonium	1944-2009
Hughes, James 'Jim'		
(nephew of T G Brookes)	Cornet	1943-53
Hughes, John (1)	Cornet/horn	1918-42
Hughes, John (2)		
(nephew of T G Brookes)	Cornet/bass	1949-53
Hughes, John (3)		
Northop Band	Cornet	1995-
Hughes, Ken	Cornet	2006-2013
Hughes, Malcolm	Trombone	1994-99
Hughes, Richard 'Dick'	Baritone	1911-54
Hughes, Sarah	Flugel	1994-
Hughes, Simon	Euphonium	2006-2009
Hughes, Susan	Baritone	
Junior band trainer		2009-14
Hughes, T	Drums	1921-22
Hughes, Thomas (1)	Horn/trombone	1929-41
Hughes, Thomas (2)		
(brother of Heulwen Hughes)	Euphonium/trombone	1998-2003
Hunt, Geraint	Horn	1940-42

Jones, David		
(brother of Michael D Jones) Horn/euph		1998-
Jones, David A	Trombone	1944-2014
Jones, David Lloyd	Cornet	1944-47
Jones, Flo	Horn	1996-2006
Jones, Francis	Euphonium	1940-42
Jones, Glyn	Cornet	1941-64
Jones, Gwyn V	Cornet	1979
Jones, J H	Horn	1916-17
Jones, John	Trombone	1979
Jones, John Llewelyn	Cornet	1917-42
Jones, Katie		
(g'dtr of Flo Jones)	Cornet	1998
Jones, Ken	Trombone	2003-
Jones, M		1975
Jones, Michael D	Cornet	
Musical Director		1998-2002
Jones, Nick		
(brother of Michael D Jones) Bass		1998-2002
Jones, Robert		
(g'son of Flo Jones)	Cornet	1998
Jones, Robert T	Cornet	1912-15
Jones, Sonia	Cornet	2004-2006
Jones, Thomas Henry 'Tommy Tinks'		
(brother of Billy Jones)	Bass	1944-2005
Jones, W J		1911-12
Jones, W J 'Billy'		
(brother of Thomas Henry Jones) Soprano/cornet		1944-2004
Jones (Johns?), Ben	Cornet/horn	1918-30
Joyce, T	Cornet	1944
Killen, Roger	Cornet/horn	1918-25
Killen, William	Cornet	1916-41
Kinsley, Tim	Bass	1990-
Kirkham, Jonathan	Horn	1999-2003
Lane, Steven	Cornet	1968-80
Lemon, Bernadette	Cornet	1998-2000
Lindon, Geoffrey	Trombone	1935-37

Lloyd, William 'Bill'	Trombone/bass	1911-25
Longworth, John	Euphonium	1940-42
Lorenz, Bram	Baritone/bass	1998-2000
Lunt, R	Baritone	1911-12
Maitland, W W	Soprano/baritone	1911-14
Marriott, Lindsay	Cornet	1979
Marston, Morgan	Cornet	2010
Marston, Will	Bass	2010
Martin, Jack F	Cornet/horn/bass	1912-23
Martin, Ronnie	Horn	1940-42
McEvoy, John James	Cornet	1998-2003
Millington, Steve Houghton Weavers	Keyboards/guitar/vocal	2011
Moise, E T		1915
Morgan, R		1967
Morgan, Robert D	Musical Director	1978-80
Morris, Malcolm	Trombone	1999
Mounfield, Don	Musical Director	1978
O'Hara, Cy	Cornet	1979-96
Oliver, Neil	Musical Director	1992
Oliver-Jones (Edwards), Bethan	Trombone	1999-
Ormrod, Jack	Bass	
Owen, Idris	Bass	1949-53
Owen, R	Cornet	1916
Owen, Tommy	Bass	1950-75
Owen, W J		1911
Palmer, A J	Trombone	1942-45
Palmer, Alan	Bass	1967-75
Parry, Ivor	Cornet/horn	1918-64
Parry, J		1911
Peachey, Alan	Horn	2007
Pearson, Joe	Percussion	2005
Pendleton (Etheridge), Julia	Cornet	1965-75
Pickersgill, Dek	Cornet	2006-2014
Price, Johnny	Horn	1940-42
Price, Peter	Bass	1913-41
Price, Selwyn	Soprano/cornet	2001-

Name	Instrument	Years
Pritchard, Vaughan	Soprano	1961-72
Quigley, Peter	Cornet	1969-71
Quiney, Eric	Cornet	1973-80
Richards, E George	Cornet	1913-17
Richards, J	Horn/baritone	1911-14
Richards, Joseph	Cornet/bass	2009-2014
Ridler, John	Cornet/flugel/bass	1949-
Roberts, ?		1925
Roberts, Dilwyn	Trombone	1961-64
Roberts, Elfed	Bass	1947-74
Roberts, Elfyn	Cornet	1943-54
Roberts, Elyn R 'Ned'	Horn/trombone	1911-54
Roberts, Evan	Soprano/cornet	1913-19
Roberts, Glyn Dryhurst		1954
Roberts, J	Trombone	1911-12
Roberts, James A 'Jim'	Euphonium	
Musical Director		1992-1998
Roberts, Joe	Cornet	2006-2011
Roberts, John K	Cornet	1979-80
Roberts, Ken	Trombone	1944-80
Roberts, Martin		1975
Roberts, Matty	Vocalist	2011
Roberts, Philip		1963
Roberts, Trevor	Cornet	1914-16
Rodrigues, John	Horn	1986-94
Rodrigues, Michelle		
(dtr of John Rodrigues)	Cornet	1986-94
Rodrigues, Robert 'Rob'		
(son of John Rodrigues)	Cornet	1987-
Royale, Roz	Vocalist	2011
Shaw, Ian		
(son of Walter Shaw)	Cornet	1972-75
Shaw, Walter	Baritone	1965-2012
Shaw (Coleman Jones), Ruth		
(dtr of Walter Shaw)	Cornet	1973-
Sheard, Melanie J	Baritone	2013-
Sherrington, Angharad	Horn	2013-

Sherwood, Peter	Euphonium	1961-64
Skelton, Billy		
(son of William Skelton)		1951
Skelton, William	Horn	
Bandmaster		1947-52
Smith, Gary A	Trombone	1972-75
Smith, Molly	Cornet	2012
Smith (Howarth), Lisa	Percussion	2005-
Stephenson, Matthew	Euphonium	1998
Thomas, Brian	Drums/percussion	2008-9
Thomas, Elgan Llŷr	Bass	2000-07
Thomas, Emlyn	Trombone	2000-2011
Thomas, Gordon	Horn	1941-42
Thomas, J R	Bass	1911-12
Thomas, Sion	Cornet	1993-99
Tocker, Arnold	Percussion	1974
Traversi, Antonio 'Tony'	Cornet	1927-45
Traversi, Francis Lucio	Cornet	
Bandmaster		1911-47
Turner, John	Trombone	1992-98
Turner, L		1915
Turner, Richard	Bass	1979-80
Tyrer, W H	Cornet/baritone	1912-20
Waddington, H		1943
Walker (Edwards), Julie		
(dtr of John J Edwards)	Horn	1971-82
Ward, Thomas	Bass	1927-54
Wareham, Deborah		
(niece of G H Brookes)	Flugel	1979
Wareham, Peter J G		
(nephew of G H Brooke)	Trombone/euph	1971-80
Westwood, Philip	Cornet	1925
Wharfe, Joanne	Cornet	1984
Wilkinson, Michael	Bass	1949-72
Wilks, Russell	Cornet	1979-80
Williams, Alex		
(son of Reg?)	Cornet/horn	1934-40

Williams, Colin	Cornet	1980
Williams, David		1911
Williams, Emlyn		
(brother of Gwilym Williams)	Cornet	1943-47
Williams, Eric	Cornet	1942-45
Williams, Gareth	Bass	2011
Williams, Gwilym		
(brother of Emlyn Williams)	Cornet	1944-47
Williams, Harry	Cornet/horn	1917-26
Williams, Isaac	Bass	1911-43
Williams, Jas		1911
Williams, John		
(brother of Roy Williams)	Horn	1956
Williams, John Wyn	Horn/euph	2001-
Williams, Keith	Cornet	1952
Williams, Lisa	Horn	1979
Williams, Mark		
(grandson of Reg Williams)	Cornet/drums	1974-80
Williams, Morris	Bass	1999
Williams, Nia Lloyd	Soprano/cornet/euph	2005-
Williams, Owen	Drums/percussion	1928-67
Williams, Peter	Drums	1911-21
Williams, Ray		1950-51
Williams, Reg O	Soprano/cornet/trombone	1912-74
Williams, Robert (1)	Bass	1911-15
Williams, Robert (2)		1943-49
Williams, Robin (Ty Isa)		1921
Williams, Robin H	Cornet/horn/euph	
Bandmaster		1913-72
Williams, Roy		
(brother of John Williams)	Cornet	1947-73
Wilson, Adam	Euphonium	2009-2012
Wolfendale, Clive E	Saxophone/clarinet	
Musical Director		2002-14
Wolfendale, Richard		
(son of Clive Wolfendale	Percussion	2012-
Wolfendale, Susan M	Trombone/percussion	2007-

Wroe, Colin	Cornet	1980
Wynne, Thomas A	Horn/euph/bass	1918-40